EARLS JUST WANNA HAVE FUN

MERRY FARMER

EARLS JUST WANNA HAVE FUN

Cover design by Erin Dameron-Hill (the miracle-worker)

ASIN: B093X811W4

Paperback ISBN: 9798532198531

Click here for a complete list of other works by Merry Farmer.

If you'd like to be the first to learn about when the next books in the series come out and more, please sign up for my newsletter here: http://eepurl.com/RQ-KX

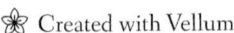 Created with Vellum

CHAPTER 1

BELFAST, IRELAND – DECEMBER 1888

*L*ady Shannon O'Shea might have been the eldest sister of a prominent earl, she might have had one sister married to an earl, one married to a marquess, and a third engaged to a duke, but she was not going to let that stop her from being a woman in her own right, and a businesswoman at that. And she most certainly wasn't about to let her brother, Lord Fergus O'Shea, trap her into a marriage the way he had with their sisters. If anyone were to steer the course of Shannon's life, it would be herself.

Although, that effort was not proceeding with the speed and ease that she would have liked it to as she stood toe to toe with one William McGinty in the backroom of McGinty's Pub in Belfast.

1

"We have been doing business by correspondence for months now, Mr. McGinty. Nearly a year," Shannon argued, fists planted on her hips, fire in her eyes.

"I have been doing business with a Mr. Shannon O'Shea for these past several months," Mr. McGinty said, arms crossed, a wry, irritating grin on his face that hinted he thought the entire argument were a joke. "Where is that Mr. O'Shea?"

"He is here, sir." Shannon stood straighter, glaring at the man with what she hoped was the full authority of her class. Not that class had done her a lick of good in her thirty years of life. "You have been doing business with me. Lady Shannon O'Shea."

"*Lady* Shannon O'Shea?" Mr. McGinty's eyes went wide and his smile grew. "You're a bloody nob on top of everything else?"

Shannon huffed out an impatient breath and pressed her fingertips to the headache forming behind her temples. "I am a businesswoman," she insisted. "I own O'Shea's Brewery, an endeavor that I started with my sisters several years ago."

"Your *sisters*?" Mr. McGinty laughed outright, clutching his belly.

"Do not mock or deride me, sir," Shannon snapped. "Yes, it is true that brewing began as a simple hobby to keep the four of us occupied, but we became quite good at it. My sisters might have moved on to other hobbies," if marriage and childrearing could even be considered

2

hobbies, "but I continued on with it. I studied every text I could get my hands on. I have corresponded with some of the largest breweries in Ireland, England, and America to perfect my art. I have experimented and made use of hops and barley from every corner of Europe. And you have been gladly purchasing and serving my beer for these many months now."

"True, but I had no idea it was made by women," Mr. McGinty laughed. "And *ladies* at that."

Shannon loathed the man for the way he snorted and guffawed. He wasn't even looking down his nose at her, as if a lady wasn't worthy of his derision.

"I will have you know," she said in a tight, clipped voice, "that women have been brewers for centuries. In the Middle Ages, the profession of brewing beer was exclusively a female endeavor. Men had nothing to do with it. They guarded their secrets and passed their art down through guilds that were tightly regulated. And now you would go against centuries of established tradition by refusing to do business with me?"

Mr. McGinty finished laughing and pulled out a handkerchief to wipe his eyes. He made a sound of enjoyment, still treating Shannon and the thing she held dearest to her heart as something funny he'd read in the papers. "Look," he said, then sniffed, put his handkerchief away, and went back to crossing his arms. "I'll continue to sell your beer in my pub, if that's what you want."

"What I want is a distribution deal so that you sell my beer in all of the pubs you own throughout the northern part of Ireland," Shannon said.

"And you think you can keep up with that sort of demand?" Mr. McGinty's brow flew up.

"Yes," Shannon insisted, "because what I also want, what we have been discussing through correspondence these many months now, is to merge your brewery with mine so that both businesses can be expanded to serve a wider area."

"No," Mr. McGinty said without so much as letting her explain her reasons. "I'm not going into business with a noblewoman."

"But you have not even read my proposal." Shannon reached into the satchel she had slung over one shoulder, intending to pull out the sheaf of papers on which her proposal and projections for profit and production were written.

"No," Mr. McGinty stopped her in a slightly more forceful voice. "I'm not interested in any of it."

"But you *were* interested," she argued. "Your letters said you were exceptionally interested."

"Interested in going into business with a *Mr.* Shannon O'Shea," Mr. McGinty matched her peevish tone.

"I *am* Shannon O'Shea," Shannon growled.

"Not the one I thought I was talking to," Mr. McGinty snapped with an air of finality. "Now, go away, your ladyship."

4

"You have not seen my proposal yet." Shannon was determined to be heard. She took the proposal pages from her satchel and shook them at Mr. McGinty. "Once you read this, I'm certain you will see—"

"I am not interested, my lady," Mr. McGinty roared, leaning closer to her. "Get out of my pub before I call the police to have you removed forcibly."

"But you haven't—"

"Go and find yourself some titled toff to marry." Mr. McGinty pointed to the back door. "Go out and buy a bunch of lovely, pretty dresses and have yourself a tea party with your friends."

"I do not have any friends," Shannon growled, glaring at the man.

He turned her words on her by leaning toward her, meeting her eyes, and saying, "Maybe that is your problem. Go!" He pointed to the door again.

Shannon squeezed the papers in her hand so hard she crumpled them. It simply wasn't fair. After all of the efforts and overtures she'd made, after all of the letters she'd written and all of the recipes she'd perfected, she was unable to do more with her business than call it a quaint little hobby, and all because she was a woman.

She glared at Mr. McGinty one more time before turning and marching out of his pub and into the alley behind it without so much as giving the man the dignity of taking her leave. Once she made it out of the alley and into the street where McGinty's pub, and several others, stood, her anger burst and she deflated into sullenness.

All over Europe and America, women were making incredible strides. They were able to attend university in many places. Women were graduating medical school and becoming doctors. Middle class women were taking jobs as secretaries and postmistresses and the like at a rate that alarmed men. There were even several enterprising women in England and America who had made fortunes for themselves as businesswomen, selling things such as cosmetics, grooming products, and household goods. Times were changing, and the future for women seemed bright.

But some dolt in a third-rate pub in Belfast wouldn't even speak to her about expanding her business so that she could join the ranks of new female entrepreneurs. It was enough to make Shannon want to shout in frustration and kick the wall of the nearest building—something she didn't do, because at least she had her dignity. So much was changing, and yet it was painfully the same as always that men insisted on only doing business with other men.

She fostered the anger boiling in her gut as she walked back to the seaside street where she'd been forced to park her wagon earlier. She'd brought sample kegs of her beer with her, and had given most of them to Mr. McGinty. More beer was brewing at home, in the cottage Shannon had shared with her sisters during the years Fergus had been in England, but a cottage industry like that would never be enough to support her business dreams.

She let out a sigh as she turned a corner and headed along the street that faced one of the docks where ferries coming from England put in. A ferry was there now, its passenger disembarking. In her heart, Shannon knew that a good half of her anger was not directed toward Mr. McGinty and his like at all, but rather was directed at her sisters. They'd had such a lively, cozy, fun life when the four of them were living at the cottage together. It had been the perfect arrangement for independent-minded women, like the four of them. As the oldest, Shannon had felt like the mother hen, taking care of Chloe, Colleen, and Marie as if they were her own.

Now they were all gone, or nearly gone. They had betrayed their solemn oath that the four of them would never marry and that they would spend their lives together, independently. Marie had her earl and was expecting her first child at Kilrea Manor. Colleen was also with child, a marchioness with a grand estate to oversee. And stary-eyed baby of the family, Chloe, was about to marry an English duke in one week. The Christmas wedding was the talk of the county, but Shannon could only think about afterward, when Chloe and her duke would move back to England to fulfill his duties.

They'd all left her, all three of them. And how long would it be until Fergus went back to England to tend to the duties that his English wife still had in managing her late husband's estates for the benefit of their son? In the blink of an eye, they would all be gone, and what would Shannon be left with?

As she drew near her wagon, a commotion from the other side of the street, near the exit of the ferry dock, caught her attention. Her heart lurched in her chest as she spotted Chloe and her groom, the Duke of Blackburn. Another man had just joined them from the ferry. Shannon was reminded that Blackburn's cousin was due to arrive that day from England, to take up duties as the duke's best man for the wedding. Well, Shannon wasn't about to let the man charge in, full of English stuffiness and superiority, and ruin her sister's wedding, her Christmas, and, if things continued on the way they had been lately, her life.

She crossed the street, shoulders squared, and approached the trio.

"That oaf at McGinty's Pub had some nerve, turning me away when he's been doing business with me by correspondence for months now," Shannon growled without a greeting. It was the only way she could think of to assert herself and let the newcomer—the something of Somebody-or-Another, if she remembered correctly—know she wasn't a woman to be trifled with. "I have half a mind to spit in the next shipment of beer I send to him, or worse."

To Shannon's surprise, the young man didn't seem at all horrified by her admittedly garish outburst. Instead, his blue eyes widened, and he swept her with an assessing look that was as heated as it was impertinent and said, "Why, hello, and aren't you lovely."

Shannon was immediately on the back foot, in spite

8

of her determination to take the upper hand in the exchange. She glared at the young man, but her rebellious heart betrayed her by speeding up and slamming against her ribs. The man was young. He must have been in his early twenties, far too young for her. He resembled his cousin in that they were both tall with dark hair and blue eyes. The young man's eyes flashed with mischief as he somehow flirted with her without saying a word.

And in the meantime, Chloe raised a hand to her mouth to hide her laughter instead of doing something to correct the whelp.

Shannon could have strangled her sister and the young lord both. She made no effort whatsoever to hide her indignation at the way she'd been greeted. "And just who in blazes do you think you are?" she asked the imp.

"Your future husband," the imp answered, dropping to one knee in a gesture that was as ridiculous as it was intriguing. "If you'll have me."

It took everything Shannon had not to burst into laughter. But no, she was annoyed by the young man's embarrassing behavior, not charmed by it. She was in the midst of a horrible day, and the whelp was only making it worse. She turned to Blackburn and asked, "Who is this ridiculous boy?"

Blackburn cleared his throat. "Colin, get up," he said out of the corner of his mouth. The young man bounded up with the sort of energy that only a man in his early twenties could have. "Lady Shannon, this is my cousin,

Lord Colin Crenshaw, Earl of Stamford," Blackburn introduced him.

Shannon blinked at the young man, her brow shooting up. "This *pup* is an earl?"

"I am," the pup said. "Though I'll be a marquess someday, when my dear father passes, if you can wait for that." He batted his eyelashes at Shannon in an overly dramatic and flirtatious manner that, again, had Shannon in danger of laughing when she didn't want to. She would not be amused by the young earl, she absolutely would not.

Blackburn cleared his throat and said, "Colin, this is Lady Shannon O'Shea, Chloe's eldest sister."

The lordling gasped as though he were on the stage. "She *does* have a sister," he said, his blue eyes going wide. "I can already tell this will be the most auspicious holiday of my life."

Shannon sighed and rolled her eyes. "And this is turning out to be the worst day of my life," she said, stepping away from them. "My wagon is parked just over there, so you will excuse me if I do not stay to indulge in chit-chat. I'm ready to go home."

"And I'm ready to go with you," the young earl said, following her.

"Truly, there is no need," Shannon assured him as she marched on, picking up her pace. "I am more than capable of seeing myself home."

"But we've only just met," the whelp said, practically

dancing by her side. "I should like to see a great deal more of you."

Shannon paused to turn to him with a flat scowl.

"Oy! You!" one of the dockworkers called after them, preventing her from saying anything. "What about all this baggage?"

"Oh, yes, my baggage," the young earl said. He flickered one eyebrow at Shannon and added, "I have quite a bit of baggage."

Shannon could only imagine what that meant.

A moment later, Blackburn called back to them, "Colin, what the devil is all this? Get back here this instant!"

There was enough emotion in Blackburn's voice that Shannon was curious. Instead of heading on to her wagon several yards away, she watched the young earl scurry back to his cousin, then followed slowly behind him to see what was going on herself.

"Ah, yes," the young man—blast, she was going to have to accept she knew him now and start calling him Stamford—blushed and ducked his head a bit as his cousin gestured to a veritable mountain of trunks, traveling bags, and cases. "I never was one to travel light."

"This looks as though it's everything you own," Blackburn said, gaping at the pile. "I thought you were only planning to stay for a fortnight."

"A fortnight," Stamford shrugged, "a month, a season. Perhaps a year."

"Dammit, man, *I'm* not even planning to stay for a

whole year," Blackburn said. His words inadvertently pierced Shannon's heart like an arrow. She glanced to Chloe, only to find her sweet youngest sister blushing modestly and looking awkward. They both knew Chloe would be off to England in no time.

"One must be prepared for anything," Stamford said.

Blackburn sighed and rubbed a hand over his face. "Well, we don't have room for all of this in the carriage. Even if we strap it all to the back and top, we'll never be able to transport it all in one go."

"Is there a place they could hold it all until we're able to send someone for it?" Chloe asked.

"I can take it," Shannon said before she could think better of the offer.

Chloe, Blackburn, and Stamford all turned to her with varying degrees of shock. Stamford's version of shock also managed to look delighted. "I think that's a splendid idea," he said. A beat later, he asked, "Are you planning to carry it all on your back?"

Shannon clenched her jaw and prayed for patience before saying, "No, I've brought the wagon today. I had a delivery to make." She needn't say more than that.

"What sort of a delivery?" Stamford asked, bouncing his way back to her like a rubber ball that a child had dropped on a slope.

Shannon had no intention of saying a word about her business.

"She's a brewer," Chloe answered for her, a teasing

light in her eyes. "She makes the most magnificent beer and sells it to pubs all across the county."

Stamford gasped. "You brew beer?" He looked at her as though she were a goddess who had just stepped down from the clouds, frothing pint in hand.

"As a business," Shannon growled. "Not for fun." Which was a ridiculous thing to say, seeing as that was exactly how she'd started the business to begin with. She glanced past Stamford to Blackburn. "I have the wagon just down there. It has plenty of room to accommodate all of Lord Stamford's things."

"How convenient," Blackburn said, a mischievous light in his expression that Shannon wasn't certain she liked. "Would you like me to have someone bring the wagon around so that the porters can load it?"

"No, my lord, I am perfectly capable of driving my own wagon," Shannon said, more irritated than she should have been, considering Blackburn was only trying to help.

She turned to head back down the street to her wagon.

"I will assist you," Stamford said, following her once again instead of staying and dealing with his own baggage as he should have.

"Truly, I don't need any assistance pulling a wagon around." Shannon tried to put him off by not looking at him as she made the comment.

But Stamford spoiled all of her intentions to ignore the man and wallow in her own bad day when he said,

"It's no problem at all. I do believe I would go to the ends of the earth for a woman as beautiful and lively as you."

Shannon stopped dead and turned to him. The whelp was smiling at her as though he believed every silly word he was saying. Oh, Lord. The next fortnight was going to be completely mad.

CHAPTER 2

*I*reland was the perfect place to run away to. Colin had known it from the moment Deane had written to him, asking him to perform the duties of best man at his wedding. He'd known in an instant that the invitation was for more than just a wedding. It was to leave his miserable old life behind and to start a new one as a new man in a new country. He'd started making plans right then and there, even though he'd still had weeks before he was due in Ireland. He'd sold off a few things that needed to be sold, bundled a few other things into storage that he wouldn't miss, and packed the things he would require into every trunk and traveling case he could find. Ireland first, and perhaps America after that, if signs pointed in that direction.

And yes, his father had made a few, snide comments about mutton-headed young men with fluff for brains packing too much for a fortnight in "bloody Ireland".

Fortunately, as the old bastard never expected much from him anyhow, he wouldn't be disappointed when he found out the truth.

Of course, his plans to run away shifted slightly the moment he'd seen the indomitable Lady Shannon O'Shea.

"Have you been driving your own wagon for long?" he asked as he strode by her side down the dockside street to where a decidedly ordinary-looking wagon waited.

A boy was minding it for her, and as soon as they approached, Lady Shannon reached into the satchel she had slung over one arm to hand the lad a coin. "It's no business of yours," Lady Shannon snapped after saying a polite thank you to the urchin, "but yes, I've been driving wagons since I was a girl. They're the best way to get around when you have actual work to do." She sent him a disparaging look, as though he hadn't known a day of work in his life.

She couldn't have been more wrong if she'd tried. Colin had done more work in his twenty-two years than most young earls and someday marquesses did in their lives. The summer he'd spent in southern France, working in the vineyard of one of his university mates, had been grueling. And he'd loved every minute of it.

"Let me help you up, then." He stepped closer to Lady Shannon with a rakish grin, grasping her around the waist and all but throwing her into the wagon's seat.

Lady Shannon shrieked, and rightly so. He was a cad who had only helped her because he wanted to feel his hands around her waist. It was a lovely waist at that—not too slight, but not too expansive. It was more than enough for a man to wrap his arms around and really feel as though he were holding something as he—

"Unhand me, you lout," Lady Shannon barked at him, scowling and interrupting his libidinous thoughts.

Colin knew that he deserved it. He also knew that the sparkle in Lady Shannon's eyes meant she wasn't as irritated with him as she let on, perhaps even to herself. She pretended as much, though, grasping the reins at the front of the wagon and nudging the horse into motion. She pulled away before Colin could hurry around and climb onto the other side of the wagon's seat, but it wasn't as though that would get rid of him. They were heading to the same place, after all.

With a laugh, he thrust his hands into his pockets and walked back up and across the street, to where Deane had enlisted the help of several porters to load his baggage onto the wagon. Dean pointed out the wagon as Lady Shannon drove to the end of the street, where there was space for her to turn around. He then turned to frown at Colin as he ambled back to join him.

"Have you vexed Lady Shannon to death already?" Deane asked, checking over his shoulder to see whether his bride-to-be could overhear them.

"She's hardly given me a chance yet," Colin said, adding, "the beautiful creature."

"Yes, well, she's a beautiful creature with years on

you who is strong-minded and has a will of her own," Deane cautioned him.

Colin let out a hum that was nearly obscene, it was so appreciative. "Exactly as I like them."

Deane shook his head at Colin. "She's about to be my sister-in-law, so have a care. I don't know what you idle young lordlings get up to these days, but please let it not be seducing innocent Irish ladies."

Colin kept his smile in place, but inwardly he seethed at everything his cousin had just said. On the one hand, he despised the term "idle rich" as though it were the gravest insult that could be hurled at a man. Idleness was all anyone ever expected of him as the son of a marquess and an earl with an estate and large income in his own right. As far back as he could remember, all anyone expected him to do was ride, shoot, play cards, and seduce women of dubious virtue. Not a single person of his acquaintance expected him to go into a profession or actually learn something at university or be a useful member of society. The closest anyone had ever come to giving him credit for being worth his salt was Deane, and now Colin had his doubts about whether his beloved cousin even took him seriously.

And the implication that he would seduce Lady Shannon with ill-intent was an insult.

He would have the very best intent when he seduced the captivating woman.

"I hereby do solemnly swear that I will not do anything to impugn your honor or that of your bride or her family while I am in Ireland," Colin promised, the cheekiness coming back to his grin as he turned to his cousin.

Deane grinned at first, but then his expression fell. "Something's off," he said. He shifted his weight, studying Colin more carefully. "Is everything all right with you, Colin?"

Prickles of guilt slithered down Colin's back. He hadn't intended to give anything away to Deane so soon.

"Everything is wonderful," Colin lied, slapping Deane's back. "My favorite cousin is about to be married, my birthday is next week, and Christmas is a few days after that. And now I'm in this beautiful country of Ireland, where the scenery is picturesque and the ladies have minds of their own."

Deane laughed at his effusiveness and thumped Colin's back in turn. "It's good to see you again," he said. "Truly. I would have paid a visit to Stonecross Abbey sooner, but there was the business of my parents' death, then the muddle in London, then you were away on the continent, then—"

"I know, I know, cuz," Colin said, clasping his hands behind his back and focusing on the way Lady Shannon looked as though she would plow through anyone who got in her way as she drove her wagon up to the side of the dock. "We're together now. That's all that matters." And they would have more time together than Deane expected, if Colin had anything to say about it.

"And how is my uncle, your father?" Deane asked, arching one eyebrow knowingly.

"As much of a bastard as ever," Colin said as Lady Shannon pulled her horse to a stop. "But forgive me if I don't elaborate. There are women present." He winked at Deane.

"Oh, Lord," Deane said under his breath, then turned to the porter to start giving instructions.

Deane knew all about Colin's brittle relationship with his father. He'd been the one to intervene between the two of them on more than one occasion, visiting Colin's childhood home of Wallingsford Park, where his father still lived and ruled the place as though he were a king and not just a marquess. In truth, if his father could have chosen his heir, Colin was certain he would have found a way to pass the marquessate to Deane instead of letting it fall on Colin's shoulders. Deane was the ideal picture of what a young nobleman should be. Colin most certainly wasn't.

"Careful with the small one up there," he said, leaping forward to oversee the porters who were transferring his things to Lady Shannon's wagon. "It has a particularly delicate wedding gift in it."

"Wedding gift?" Deane asked, one eyebrow raised, as though Colin's gift might bite.

"You'll see in good time," Colin told him.

He turned to wink at Lady Shannon—who was ostensibly privy to the conversation, since she'd hopped down from the wagon to open the back for the porters. As soon as Lady Shannon caught the gesture, her lips pursed, and a lovely shade of pink flooded her cheeks. She truly was a beauty, but the sort that likely didn't realize her own charm. She had flame-red hair—like her sister, Deane's bride—that was caught up in a fashionable style with a pert, green hat that matched her serviceable outfit perched on top. Her appearance would have been stern and businesslike, but for the strands of hair that had pulled out of their style and the slight smudge on the arm of the grey wool coat that covered her, but did little to hide her shape. Best of all, though, were the woman's brilliant, green eyes that seemed to bore right into Colin's soul.

"Let me help you with that," Colin said—not to Lady Shannon, but to the porter who was attempting to lift one of his larger, heavier chests.

The porter grunted as Colin stooped to grasp one of the trunk's handles, then sent Colin a look as though he were impressed as the two of them carried the trunk to the back of the wagon. Colin ignored all rules of class and propriety and helped the porters load his things. He enjoyed the stretch and strain of his muscles as he did real work, and the surprised look Deane sent him wasn't half bad either.

"You don't have to do that, my lord," the head porter told him as Colin continued to haul his own baggage. The poor man looked almost offended that a lord would lift a finger to help load a wagon.

"Nonsense," Colin told the man. "I am attempting to

impress a young lady," he pretended to whisper while actually speaking loud enough for everyone to hear.

Deane hid a chuckle behind his hand. Lady Shannon glared mutinously at him. Lady Chloe—who had come back to seeing to some sort of business with the carriage—lifted to her toes and whispered something in Deane's ear, grinning at her sister as she did. Deane laughed and nodded at whatever it was. Lady Shannon went as stiff as a board as she resumed her place in the seat of her wagon, as if she knew her sister were making a joke at her expense.

"That's all of it," the head porter said, gesturing for his men to close up the back of the wagon.

"Excellent," Colin said, reaching into his coat to take out his wallet, then handing the head porter an exorbitantly large note in thanks. "Wish me luck," he added with a wink, nodding sideways at Lady Shannon.

The porter merely laughed as Colin strode up to the front of the wagon.

"There's plenty of room for you in the carriage," Deane said as Colin grabbed hold of the side of the wagon and prepared to hoist himself into the seat beside Lady Shannon. He likely already guessed what Colin had in mind.

"I wouldn't think of leaving Lady Shannon alone with my burdens," Colin said, bounding up into the wagon and plopping on the seat beside the irritated woman. "Besides, isn't the Irish countryside full of marauders and other murderous sorts who are just itching to get their hands on beautiful, Protestant ladies?"

"Not for a decade or more," Lady Shannon grumbled. "So you can get down and drive with your cousin."

"I'm perfectly happy where I am," Colin beamed at her.

Lady Shannon shook her head, but the flush remained on her cheeks, and it wasn't a flush of irritation.

"He's staying at Kilrea Manor with me," Deane told Lady Shannon. "We've a call to pay on the way home, so I trust you know the way on your own."

"I do, my lord," Lady Shannon said, picking up the reins again. "I've quite a bit more work to do myself today, so we won't be lingering over any sort of conversation." She sent a pointed look Colin's way.

If Lady Shannon thought they wouldn't be lingering and getting to know each other a great deal better, she had another think coming.

The traffic near the dock was such that it took them a bit before they could move more than a few yards at a time on their way to the road heading out of town. Colin could see that Lady Shannon needed her full attention to steer through it all safely. He didn't bother her more than to compliment her on her handling of the horse or to point out obstacles she might not have been aware of.

Once they were on the road outside of the bustling city, heading across winter-dormant fields and past trees that had lost all their leaves for the season, Colin felt no qualms about pestering the stuffing out of his beautiful driver.

"Have you always been a fabulous beauty or is it something you've cultivated with age?" he asked, hoping she would be as bothered by his mention of age as she was flattered by his comment about her beauty.

She glanced sideways at him and fired back with, "Have you always been a blithering fool or is that something your nanny taught you?"

Colin burst out laughing. More than that, his trousers tightened noticeably. "I developed those skills all on my own, in spite of everyone's best efforts to make me into who they wanted me to be," he said. He didn't expect the faint hint of bitterness that leaked into his tone.

Lady Shannon must have caught it. She turned her head a bit more to stare at him.

Colin wasn't about to ruin a perfectly lovely afternoon with seriousness, so he asked, "Did you teach yourself to make beer or did you have an instructor?"

"I taught myself through a mail-order course and other instructional books," she said, her back going straight as she gazed forward across the landscape.

"I see," Colin said, his mouth twitching into a grin. "And do you enjoy sampling the fruits of your labor?"

"Excessively," Lady Shannon replied with dry flatness, as if she saw through what he was asking. "I host drunken bacchanals at the cottage where my brewery is set up all the time."

"Marvelous." Colin played along with her humorless ribbing. "Can I come to your next one? I would gladly stand in as Bacchus, the god of wine. I cut a dashing figure when I'm wearing nothing but a loincloth."

Lady Shannon's eyes went wide, and she turned her head to gape at him. Of course, her incredulous look wasn't helped at all when she inadvertently swept a look across his body. Her cheeks went even pinker. "Impudent boy," she hissed.

"I will have you know that I'm no boy," Colin insisted. "I am twenty-two, a graduate of Cambridge, a member of the House of Lords, and I spent an entire summer in the south of France last year."

"Sampling French wine, no doubt," Lady Shannon muttered, "and irritating unsuspecting Frenchwomen by telling them they were beautiful."

"I did sample French wine," Colin said, uncertain why her comments—which he'd more or less asked for by the way he teased her—put him on the defensive, "but only because I helped in the process of making it. I worked in the vineyard, tending and harvesting the grapes."

Lady Shannon's frown shifted into a look of surprise.

"And I did not irritate the Frenchwomen I wooed and worshiped them and showed them a good time," Colin went on, perhaps unwisely.

"I should have known you were a rake as well as a rogue," Lady Shannon huffed, snapping the reins over her horse's back to get it to move faster.

"I am a brilliant and considerate lover," Colin bragged, teasing Lady Shannon with a lascivious look.

Lady Shannon gaped at him. "I am astounded, nay, horrified that you would brag so freely about such things, and in the company of a lady."

Colin grinned at her shock, suspecting it was only skin deep. "I'm not ashamed to admit my strengths, whether society finds it shocking or not. I've never had to coerce anyone into my bed or engage in any sort of silliness, like the kind my cousin found himself embroiled in last year in London. I simply worked in the fields with the other laborers, enjoyed food, song, and wine at the end of the day, and ended up in bed with whichever of the deserving young women who worked alongside the men wanted me on any given night."

It had been an enjoyable, unencumbered way to spend a summer, too. Summer laborers had a different sort of code that they lived by—one that was all about work and enjoyment, not idleness, games, and subterfuge. He longed for that sort of simple life again. It had been as intoxicating as the wine they produced by the end of his time in France.

He realized he'd been silent too long when he caught Lady Shannon staring at him. "And what about high society and London balls?" she asked him. "What about winning or losing it all at the card table or the racetrack? What about nabbing the perfect debutante to take on the duties of being your countess and siring the next Earl of Stamford?"

"God, what a boring life that would be," Colin answered, leaning back against the wagon's seat and staring up at the clouds skittering across the Irish sky, holding one hand to his hat to keep it from falling off.

Lady Shannon's expression had shifted subtly but inexorably to curiosity as she watched him. "You aren't inclined to a life of idleness and fun?"

Colin winced outright. "Do you know, that is my least favorite word in the English language."

"What, 'fun'?" Lady Shannon blinked at him.

Colin laughed. "Heavens, no. I love a bit of fun as much as the next man. I hate the word 'idle'."

"Isn't that what you are supposed to be?" she asked, one eyebrow raised.

"Far from it."

For a moment, the pang of who everyone thought he was supposed to be hit him so hard that all he could do was stare straight ahead—as Lady Shannon had returned to doing—and envision the long, dull road of his future as the Earl of Stamford, and someday the Marquess of Wallingsford, stretching out before him. It was exactly as Lady Shannon had hinted—a well-positioned wife he didn't love, as his father didn't love his mother, children he felt alienated from, as his father was alienated from him, and nothing but idle conversations, idle pastimes, and idle friendships with men he didn't particularly like, but who had the right titles.

But that was all behind him now. He glanced over his shoulder at all of his worldly belongings piled into the back of the wagon. Deane had provided him with a way out, and he was going to take it.

"So why aren't you married, Lady Shannon?" he asked the cheekiest question he could, deliberately, so that Lady Shannon would fly into another fit so that he could again bask in her indignation and her strength.

She surprised him by answering, "Because I would rather birth and raise a business than children. I would rather grow a brewing empire than roses in a garden, and I would rather the fruits of my labor entertain pub-goers across Ireland than host tea parties in the manicured gardens of some dozy country estate owned by a man my brother trapped me into marrying."

Colin's eyebrows rose so quickly that he thought they might fly right off his head. "My, my, Lady Shannon. That is ambitious."

"I have a right to be ambitious." She raised her voice as though he had told her she shouldn't be. Which led Colin to wonder what the woman's day had been like before she'd stormed into his life, like Athena entering the field of battle. "I have a right to grow a business that I have put thought and effort into," she went on. "I have a right to expand and take on as much as any man takes on."

"Then why don't you?" Colin asked with a shrug. He leaned his elbows against the top of the wagon seat, slouching like a laborer on his way back from the fields, his boots propped up on the footboard in front of him. "Why don't you create a brewing empire?"

"Because that blasted fool, McGinty, refuses to do business with a woman," Lady Shannon growled. "Because every promise and plan he made me in the last year vanished like a puff of smoke when he discovered the Shannon O'Shea he'd been corresponding with was a woman and not a man."

"The bastard," Colin gasped on her behalf. "How dare he?"

"Oh, he can dare, all right," she said, rolling her eyes at him. "All you men ever do is dare. At the expense of women. I'd wager I know more about brewing and beer than most of the men in County Antrim."

"Then go into business for yourself," Colin said, smiling as he watched her fuming over something that wasn't him.

"That's what I've been trying to do for months now," she sighed. "But McGinty is an ass, O'Donnell was a prick, and Dylan wouldn't even take a meeting with me when he discovered I am a woman."

Colin's brow shot up all over again. "You've approached all those men about going into business?"

"And more besides," she growled. "I'm supposed to meet with a Mr. Michael Doherty in a few days. He has a small brewery and a handful of pubs, and I've heard he's looking to expand."

"That's a good thing, then," Colin said.

She sent him a frustrated, sideways look. "What do you think is going to happen the moment Doherty lays eyes on me?" she asked.

Colin grinned from ear to ear. "He will see how beautiful and fiery you are. He'll see that you have the determination of a dozen men, and that he'd be a fool not to lay his heart at your feet and do whatever you tell him to do."

Lady Shannon started, as though that wasn't the answer she'd expected. In fact, Colin had no idea he was about to lay his heart on the line like that until it'd happened. Lady Shannon was magnificent. Better by far than any of the strapping French women who had grabbed him by his suspenders after a long day of work, pushed him onto his back in their beds, and ridden him like he was a prized stallion.

He blinked out of his lascivious thoughts when he realized Lady Shannon's cheeks had gone as red as apples and her eyes glittered, as though she knew exactly what he was thinking. But she cleared her throat and said, "You are wrong. Doherty will be just like the others. He'll see I'm a woman and he'll turn me away."

"What if you weren't a woman," Colin said, even though it was a ridiculous notion. Lady Shannon was absolutely a woman, and a delicious one at that.

She laughed at the notion, as well she should. "Would that were even possible."

"Well, what if you had a man with you when you went to negotiate?" he asked.

She opened her mouth to reply, but stopped.

She glanced to him again, sparks in her eyes.

"What *if* I had a man with me when I went to negotiate?" She repeated his question with a wicked lilt to her voice. "What if that man pretended to be my business partner? What if he let me conduct most of the negotiations, but stepped in when he needed to as reassurance, from one man to another."

Colin jerked to sit straight, his heart pounding against his ribs. "I'll do it," he blurted, more excited than he'd been since returning from France. "I will absolutely do it. I'll go to your meeting and be as silent as the tomb, or I'll learn whatever lines you tell me and speak for you. I'll do whatever you tell me to, during the meeting and after. I love it when women tell me what to do."

He knew he'd said too much when Lady Shannon's eyes went round. The woman was no innocent, fainting violet. Considering what he'd confessed to her just a few minutes before, he figured she was savvy enough to know the double meaning in his words. Strangely, though, he didn't mind one bit.

She was silent for a few more moments before saying, "That's Kilrea Manor ahead. I'll drop you and your things off there."

"And then tell me when we will set off to have this meeting with one Mr. Michael Doherty?" Colin asked.

Lady Shannon frowned. She pursed her lips. She let out a breath through her nose. She stared straight ahead, then peeked at him, then stared straight ahead again. She clenched her jaw and made a small noise of frustration.

Then she turned to him and said, "Alright, you can come with me."

*L*ord Colin Crenshaw, Earl of Stamford was the very last thing Shannon needed in her life when the whole thing hung in such precarious balance. And yet, from the moment she dropped him off at Kilrea Manor and saw to it that his ridiculously large amount of possessions were unloaded from her cart, from the moment she drove on to the cottage and left the brash, wicked, scandalous, handsome young lordling behind her, she couldn't stop thinking about him.

What sort of earl worth his salt spoke so openly and freely about the wickedness of his past? The man was barely old enough to have a past in the first place. How was it humanly possible for a lord like that to have no shame and no qualms at all about telling her of his past lovers, even if it was just in passing? And how could the young whelp seem so pleased with himself...while at the same time seeming so restless?

Shannon was determined not to think about him as she dove into work, preparing her latest batch of beer to take with her to the meeting with Mr. Doherty, and while helping Chloe with wedding preparations. It wasn't as though she had a single bit of space in her thoughts for a man like Lord Stamford. He was just another arrogant young nobleman with too much time on his hands and a title and wealth that allowed him to get into trouble. And besides, he was eight years younger than her. That should mean something.

All that didn't stop her from asking Chloe, "Did you know that Lord Stamford worked at a vineyard in France last summer?" as they drove to Kilrea Manor in the wagon the day of the meeting with Doherty.

"Did he?" Chloe asked, blinking in surprise. "Deane hasn't mentioned anything about it."

"Apparently, he spent an entire summer working among the vines, like a common laborer," Shannon said, tilting her head up as if she didn't approve as she spoke, but secretly finding the whole idea fascinating.

"I had no idea," Chloe said. "I'm not convinced that Deane knows either, although I'm certain he must. He and Colin are close."

Shannon merely hummed in response, pretending she wasn't interested. Inwardly, she wondered how many other things Blackburn knew about his cousin...and whether he was willing to share.

"I suppose it makes sense, though," Chloe went on.

"Colin is a Sagittarius, after all. They can be quite whimsical."

Shannon sent her sister a disapproving, sideways look. "You shouldn't refer to him by his given name. You should be calling him Stamford."

"But why?" Chloe blinked a little too innocently at Shannon, as if she knew something. "He's more like a brother to Deane than a cousin, which means he's more like a brother to me."

Something about the subtle implication of Chloe's words and the teasing grin her sister wore made Shannon squirm on the wagon's seat. She even tapped the reins over the horse's back to get it to hurry on so that the conversation would end faster.

"I noticed that you and Colin got along quite well when you met the other day," Chloe said in a needling voice.

"We did not," Shannon huffed.

Chloe ignored her. "Colin says that the two of you enjoyed quite a lovely drive home, and that he'll be driving out with you this morning as well."

"On business," Shannon insisted, sending her sister a flat look. "Stamford is helping me with business." She sighed, letting out her frustrations, and went on with, "I've taken meetings with half a dozen pub owners and brewers in the last month, but none of them will do business with a woman. Even though they agree that my product is exceptional and that their facilities would be capable of producing it in larger batches."

"Oh, Shannon, I'm sorry." Chloe dropped her teasing and turned genuinely sympathetic. "I know how hard you've worked on that business."

"And now I need the likes of Lord Stamford to accompany me to a meeting just so that I'm not turned away the moment the man I've been doing business with for months discovers I'm a woman."

"That must be a hard blow," Chloe sighed. She brightened a moment later as they made their final approach up the drive of Kilrea Manor and spotted Lord Stamford waiting for them. "But look, there's your champion now."

Shannon rolled her eyes at Chloe even as a pleased shiver ran through her. She rejected the feelings that came with sighting Colin—that was, Lord Stamford—leaning against the side of Kilrea Manor's front door, hands in his pockets, as though he were some sort of day laborer lounging against the side of a pool hall. He was all mischief and beauty and easy manner, and as soon as Shannon pulled the wagon to a stop at the base of the manor's front stairs, he pushed away from the door and beamed at Shannon as though she had brought the moon with her.

"There's my bride-to-be," he said, hopping jauntily down the stairs to help Chloe out of the wagon. He glanced past Chloe to wink at Shannon.

"In what fantasy world am I your bride-to-be?" Shannon growled at him.

"I proposed to you the other day, don't you remember?" Colin—no, Stamford, blast it—asked as he made certain Chloe had her feet on the ground. "You never answered me," he went on, practically leaping up to the wagon's seat to take Chloe's place. "And seeing as silence means consent, you are my beautiful, fiery bride-to-be."

"I am nothing of the sort," Shannon snapped, glaring at Chloe—who had just slapped a hand over her mouth to stop herself from giggling. "We are embarking on a matter of business only, and I will thank you to remember that."

"Oh, I remember, all right," Colin said, turning to make a giddy face at Chloe.

Chloe giggled all the more. "Have a lovely *business* outing," she told the two of them as she stepped up onto the stairs, then waved as Shannon nudged the horse into motion.

"Please do not give my sister any ideas that she shouldn't have, particularly about the two of us," she said in a clipped voice as they headed back down the drive and along the road toward Belfast. As pleased as she was to have a meeting with another prominent pub owner in a city as big as Belfast, she dreaded how long it would take to drive there. With Colin.

No, Stamford.

Oh, hell. She was never going to be able to think of him as anything less than Colin now.

"So you admit there is a two of us?" Colin asked, slouching against the wagon seat and putting one of his boots up on the footboard, as he had the other day. The posture did rather make him look as though he should be riding in a cart back from a day tending grape vines and less like an earl.

"There is no such thing," Shannon said. "There is only me trying to make a name for myself in the world of business—a world which is hostile toward the fairer sex—and you coming along as a necessary prop."

"So I am a prop now?" Colin brightened at the idea, for some ridiculous reason.

"You are, my lord," Shannon said, feeling awkward for addressing him so formally. "I am quite certain you are used to being one as well."

"Me? Used to being a prop?" He looked genuinely confused and sat straighter. "Explain."

"Isn't that what all young noblemen are?" she asked, turning her horse onto a larger road that wound over winter hills and frosted landscapes, the sea as unchangeable as ever, visible in the distance. "Mere props to hold up their miscreant chums? Decorations to grace box seats at Covent Garden and at Ascot?"

"I detest horse racing," Colin said, making a face. "It's cruel for the horses and turns those watching it into asses."

Shannon's brow shot up. She stole a peek at him, but snapped her gaze forward as soon as she caught him staring at her with an impish grin.

"I love the theater, though," he went on. "It's grand fun. I try to see every new show I can." He paused, then nudged her arm and asked, "Do you like the theater?"

"I've never been," Shannon admitted. "At least, not to a professional production in a city theater."

"Never?" Colin gaped at her. "Well, we must honeymoon in London, at least for a start, and I'll take you to a play. There's a brilliant young playwright named Niall Cristofori whose work I simply adore. You'll like him."

"I will not," Shannon said, no idea why she felt the compulsion to be so contrary.

Colin laughed as though he knew what game she was playing. "I'll take you to all the theaters in London, and when we've exhausted those, we'll travel on to Paris and go to the ballet."

"Yes, and I suppose a young lordling like you is quite well known in all of the theaters and music halls of Paris," Shannon scoffed. "Likely well known by all of the actresses and ballerinas as well, since you admit to taking lovers so freely."

"Good Lord, Lady Shannon," Colin laughed. "You do make a lot of assumptions."

Heat flooded Shannon's face, and she stole a sheepish, sideways glance at him. "There is a type," she said.

"There is," Colin admitted with a nod. "I know it well. The titled young lord who only wants to have fun. I have had that mantel foisted upon me from the time I was out of short pants."

The edge of frustration in Colin's voice gave Shannon pause. She stole another peek at him and found him gazing straight ahead of them, a pinched look on his face. "I am sorry," she apologized. "It was wrong of me to make assumptions, particularly when assumptions are made about me so often, and to my detriment."

"Oh?" Colin sat straighter again. "What sort of assumptions do people make about you?"

The road they traveled along had more traffic than the lazy country road they'd set out on. Shannon was all too aware of the other carriages, carts, and buggies on their way to Belfast around them. She couldn't deny Colin an answer, though, but she would keep her voice down, just in case they were overheard.

"Everyone assumes that, as the sister of an earl, all I want is to snag a rich, tilted husband and to live out the rest of my days as a wife and mother and a prominent figure in society." She hesitated for a moment, then added, "Like my sisters."

"Yes, your sisters have done quite well for themselves," Colin said. There was something rote and practiced about the way he spoke, as though he were deliberately parroting things that were generally said whenever a woman made a good match.

"They've abandoned the principles we all claimed to espouse just a few short years ago," Shannon grumbled before she could stop herself.

She hadn't meant to say something so intimate, and when Colin's brow flew up and he sat straighter, she wished she hadn't said it at all.

"What are these principles of which you speak?" he asked with exaggerated interest.

"Nothing," Shannon said. "Never mind. We should

talk about my business so that you will know what to say if called upon."

"Yes, yes, of course," he said, then rushed right on to repeat, "What principles?"

"My brewing operation is small at the moment, but it could easily be scaled into something larger," Shannon said deliberately. "I currently have two large vats for brewing two different types of beer at a time, but with larger equipment and a more expansive facility, I estimate that I could produce enough beer weekly to supply two dozen pubs at least."

"And is that part of your principles?" Colin leaned closer to her, his eyes dancing with mischief.

Shannon blew out a breath through her nose. "I have spoken to my suppliers about increasing my purchases, and the important ones are more than able to comply," she went on. "The farmer I work with who grows the best hops in Ireland is particularly interested in forming an exclusivity agreement, if I am able to purchase his entire crop every year."

"In a way that conforms to these principles of yours," Colin said, scooting closer to her.

Shannon sent him what she hoped was a withering, sideways look, but Colin just kept beaming at her.

"Barley is easier to come by, but I have found a farmer in Shropshire whose produce is second to none," she went on. "He, too, would be interested in an exclusivity agreement. Which is why it is so vital for me to find a business partner and financial backer with the capital to invest in these things."

"And who will conform to your principles," Colin added. "Which I am still waiting to hear about."

"You, sir, are a menace," Shannon huffed at him.

It just so happened that she made her comment right as they passed a wagon heading in the other direction. That wagon's driver glared at her as though she'd insulted him.

"Don't worry," Colin told the man, twisting in his seat to call after him. "She's talking about me." He turned back to Shannon with a grin as broad as the Irish coast. "Because I am not going to give up until she tells me what these principles that her sisters betrayed are."

"They didn't betray them," Shannon said, feeling suddenly wistful. "They let themselves fall victim to our brother's scheme to marry us all off, and without much of a fight, if you ask me."

"Ah. I see," Colin said, slouching against the wagon's seat again.

The way he grinned at her irritated Shannon to no end. "What do you see?" she asked with a frown.

"You're the eldest, are you not?" he asked.

"I am," Shannon said cautiously, feeling as though he was setting her up to take a fall.

"You're sad because all of the little chickees have left the nest and you've no one left to care for."

His words were gently spoken, but they hit Shannon as though he'd wielded them like a cudgel. "That is not

41

true," she lied. "I am happy for my sisters. They are happy with their lives. Everyone is happy."

"So very happy," Colin added, once again with that sharp edge to his voice that intrigued her. When Shannon peeked sideways at him—which was becoming more difficult as they grew closer to Belfast and driving required her full attention—he was watching her with a look of heated sympathy. "You can take care of me, if you'd like," he said with a lazy grin that stirred Shannon's blood. "If you ask my cousin, he'd tell you I require quite a great deal of taking care of. I promise I'll do everything you tell me to." He flickered an eyebrow at her to emphasize his point.

Shannon huffed out a breath and sat straighter, fighting the swirls of arousal that his expression sent through her. He was a cad and a bounder, whether he admitted as much to himself and others or not. He would have to be in order to be able to wheedle the kinds of confessions she'd made out of her. And if she was attracted to him as a man, that was only because he was objectively handsome and had an easy manner. Not because the suggestive way he spoke conjured up feelings in her that she'd never been able to entertain before.

"The only thing I need you to do," she said, then had to clear her throat, as her voice came out raspy and hoarse, "is to stand by my side being male when I speak with Mr. Doherty."

Colin perked up, sitting straighter. "I don't think

anyone has ever asked me just to stand there being male before."

"There is a first time for everything," Shannon drawled, sending him a sideways smirk. She sucked in a breath when he returned her comment with a flirty glance, then said, "I sincerely hope that Mr. Doherty will allow me to talk and explain all of the specifics of my brewery and my plans. I also have a written proposal in my satchel there."

"You come prepared, I see," Colin said, picking up the satchel from under the wagon's seat and searching for the proposal.

"One must always be prepared in business," Shannon said. "That is how one succeeds."

"One is decidedly lovely when she is talking business," he said in an overly amorous voice.

"For heaven's sake, Colin, pay attention," she snapped.

Only when Colin grinned warmly and said, "Yes, Shannon," did she realize she'd accidentally called him by his given name.

She blew out a breath in frustration and pressed her lips together. The cat was out of the bag now, and judging by the cheeky way Colin was gazing at her, there would be no putting it back in.

"This is important to me," she emphasized, stealing another sideways glance. "So pay attention and learn everything you will need to know if Mr. Doherty should ask you questions."

They spent the rest of the drive into Belfast going over every detail of Shannon's brewing business. Colin glanced over her written proposal as she spoke, but she couldn't tell if he was taking any of the information in. He seemed far more interested in grinning at her and making every third thing she said into some sort of scandalous inuendo. In all her life, Shannon had never known any young man so open with his opinions, or so badly in need of a thorough spanking. Her face went red as that thought suggested itself to her. She was absolutely not that kind of woman.

But the way Colin kept grinning at her made her consider changing.

"Mr. Doherty kindly informed me that I can park my wagon in his mews," she explained an hour later to a gruff man who seemed intent on blocking her from the mews behind a row of shops and pubs in the heart of Belfast. "He is expecting me, Shannon O'Shea."

The man looked suspicious for a moment, but allowed her to drive on into the mews after nodding to Colin.

"You see the sort of prejudice I am up against?" Shannon whispered as she drew the horse around to a suitable spot.

"Not the sort of thing I would wish for you to be up against," Colin said with a mock serious frown.

Shannon rolled her eyes at him as she tied the reins, then set to work gathering her things. Colin seemed intent on proving his point, though, as he leapt down from the wagon, then raced around to hold up his hands, as though he would help her down.

"I do not need your help," she insisted.

"I thought me helping you was the entire point of me accompanying you on this foray," Colin sassed back to her.

He didn't wait for her to reply. She started to climb down from the wagon and he reached for her, grabbing her around the waist and lifting her the rest of the way down. It was no surprise at all to Shannon that she ended up in his arms, held firmly against him as he gazed wickedly into her eyes. His hands lingered far longer than they should have on her waist.

"What are you doing?" she asked him in a no-nonsense voice.

"Being male," he answered, holding her tighter still. "I told you, I'm quite good at it."

It took everything Shannon had not to laugh at him. Her heart ran riot against her ribs and her legs didn't seem to want to support her properly. She pushed away from him with a frown that was mostly for herself and her own, silly reactions, but she missed being in his arms as soon as she wasn't any longer.

"Look sharp, Lord Stamford," she told him over her shoulder as she marched away from him, toward the alley that would take her back to the street. "We have a business meeting to attend."

CHAPTER 4

*I*reland. Colin was most definitely running away to Ireland. He'd considered America when he'd packed up all of his things and left home, but he was certain now that his destiny lay in Ireland. More specifically, his destiny lay with Shannon O'Shea. He was absolutely going to marry the woman. He adored her.

"Whatever you do," Shannon instructed him as they strode up the street toward Doherty's Pub, side by side, Colin's insides tumbling around like a colt in spring, "do not stand out right from the start or do anything that will make Mr. Doherty think you are the one in charge of this business."

"Right." Colin nodded. "I won't. I am only here to be male. The limelight is all yours."

And it was. A thousand times over, it was. Shannon shone like the sun when she took charge and spoke about her business. He'd been captivated through the whole ride to Belfast as she rattled off facts and figures about the making of beer that he hadn't even dreamed of. She was so confident, so determined. It gave him serious ideas about all the ways he could worship that confidence in a horizontal position and unfurl all of her pent-up energy.

"Chances are that Mr. Doherty will assume you are the one he will be speaking with today no matter what we do," Shannon said with too much bitter resignation in her voice.

"But I will defer to you in everything," Colin finished her thought for her. "I am your prop, my lady," he said, admittedly too giddily. "I am putty in your hands, your servant to command."

They'd reached the door to the pub, and Shannon turned to him with a withering look...that had exactly the opposite effect. He was so aroused by everything about Shannon that he would be walking funny for the rest of the afternoon.

He took her look as the scolding it was meant to be and jumped ahead of her to hold open the door. Shannon drew in a breath as if going into battle, tilted her head up proudly, and marched into the pub. It was all Colin could do not to bounce and jump like a newborn lamb as he followed her.

Shannon drew the attention of everyone in the pub from the moment she first entered. It was midday and hardly the time for patrons to be drunk or raucous. Most of the gentlemen in the establishment looked to be there only to enjoy lunch or to pass time with a friend or two.

The atmosphere was jolly and warm, and everything came to an abrupt stop as Shannon made her way well into the pub. She was the only woman there, and noticeably so.

"Can I help you, miss?" the bartender asked. He was a strapping man with a fashionably large moustache and a belly to match, and he seemed amused that Shannon was there at all.

"I have an appointment with Mr. Doherty," Shannon announced, as bold as you please. Colin fell more deeply in love with her by the second.

The bartender looked dubious, but sent the boy who was polishing pint glasses behind him scurrying into the back room.

A few moments later, the boy returned, leading a tall, middle-aged fellow that looked more like a gentleman than the sort of bloke who would pass time in his own pub.

"Shannon O'Shea?" he asked, sending a confused look to Colin, then Shannon, then glancing back to Colin again.

Colin stood half a step behind Shannon, and when the man—who he assumed was Doherty—looked confused, Colin silently raised a hand to point at Shannon.

Doherty focused on Shannon again just in time for Shannon to step forward, her hand outstretched.

"Mr. Doherty, we meet at last," Shannon said, shaking the man's hand with enthusiasm that surprised Colin, and all of the rest of the men in the pub.

"*Miss* O'Shea?" Doherty asked hesitantly. He glanced to Colin again and said, "I didn't realize the 'S. O'Shea' I've been dealing with these past few months is a woman."

"A lady at that," Colin added proudly.

Doherty's eyes went wide, and he dropped Shannon's hand, flustered.

Shannon twisted to glare at Colin, as if reminding him of his orders to be quiet.

"Well, er, perhaps we should continue this in my office in the back," Doherty said, then cleared his throat, then gestured awkwardly for Shannon and Colin to follow him.

They followed, and Colin noted that as soon as they ducked into the back of the pub, the place burst into chatter and buzz, most likely about Shannon and what she could possibly be doing there.

Doherty led them through a storage room and past a kitchen to a narrow set of stairs. They continued up to an office on the first floor that was stacked with crates and cabinets, and everything else Colin would have imagined a business office to contain. There was even a small desk, but instead of sitting at it—as Colin's father sat behind his massive, mahogany thing whenever he wished to pass judgement on his errant son, or the rest of the family—he merely leaned against it.

"You have me confused, Miss—er, Lady O'Shea,"

Doherty said.

"Miss O'Shea is adequate for the purposes of business," Shannon said. She shifted to the side somewhat and gestured toward Colin. "Allow me to introduce my associate, Mr. Colin Crenshaw."

Colin's mouth twitched as she completely left out his title. He'd never been addressed without his title before. It was almost as though he was introduced properly for the first time. He reached for Mr. Doherty's hand, shook it, and said, "How do you do?"

"Well, sir," Doherty said, then glanced in confusion between him and Shannon. "You have me on the back foot. Who have I been corresponding with? And who is it who owns O'Shea Brewery?"

Colin would have thought it'd be dead obvious from the name alone, but apparently names were not Doherty's strong suit.

"The business is mine, Mr. Doherty," Shannon said, taking charge and making Colin's heart sing. "I am the owner and operator of O'Shea's Brewery, and I've come to you today to discuss a merger of our two enterprises. Now, as you can see, I have put together a proposal that I believe you will find most intriguing." She reached into her satchel and handed Doherty the proposal Colin had read on the ride over.

Colin clasped his hands meekly behind his back and watched the scene unfold with a grin. Shannon absolutely knew what she was doing down to the last detail. Her proposal was excellent—well-written, and insightful.

Doherty would be a fool not to leap into business with her.

But the blighter winced at the proposal instead of reading it and said, "You must understand my hesitation, Miss O'Shea. Most of the pubs in Belfast forbid women from entering, let alone doing business with pub owners."

"I would not need to enter the premises to supply beer, Mr. Doherty," Shannon insisted, undeterred. "I believe your patrons have been enjoying the small batches of beer that I've been able to supply you with thus far."

"They have," Doherty said, scratching his head and staring at the proposal, still without reading it. "I've tried it myself. It's dam—it's very good beer."

Colin's mouth twitched at the man's reticence to use foul language in front of Shannon. He had a feeling Shannon was capable of speech as colorful as that of any pirate, if put to the test.

"It is excellent beer," Shannon said. "I've perfected the recipes for several varieties myself over the past year and more. I only use the finest ingredients, and I have suppliers who would—"

"The problem isn't the beer," Doherty cut her off.

"Then what is the problem," Shannon asked, clipping each and every syllable.

Doherty looked at her as though she knew what the problem was as much as he did. "I cannot do business with a woman."

"Why not?" Shannon asked, standing straighter and

speaking forcefully.

"My lady, you know why," Doherty said. He tried to hand the proposal back, but Shannon wouldn't take it.

"Sir, my sex and my family connections have nothing to do with the quality of my beer, which you yourself have sampled and enjoyed," Shannon said. "I cannot produce enough on my own to meet all of your distribution needs, but if we combined your current brewing operation and equipment with my recipe and suppliers, we could—"

"Family," Doherty said, one eyebrow raised. "Hold on, you aren't a member of *the* O'Shea family, are you? Lord Fergus O'Shea?"

"He is my brother," Shannon said. Colin caught the sink of defeat in the way her shoulders angled down and her head bowed slightly.

"So your sister is the one marrying that duke," Doherty went on. "I received an invitation to that wedding. My wife has some connection to the whole thing, I think. It's the social event of the Christmas season."

"Yes, I am very happy for my sister's upcoming nuptials," Shannon said impatiently, "but I came here today to discuss business with you, not to pay a social call."

"And I appreciate that, Lady O'Shea, but I can't—"

"The fact that Miss O'Shea is a woman and the sister of an earl has no bearing whatsoever on her business," Colin cut in. He understood completely now why

Shannon had wanted him there with her. Horrible though it was, she truly wouldn't be able to get anything done without a man by her side.

"Do you have something to add, Mr. Crenshaw?" Doherty asked, handing the proposal to Colin.

"You need to keep that, and you need to read it," Colin said, refusing to take it. "An opportunity is being presented to you today that could take your pubs from simple meeting places for working men in need of refreshment at the end of a long day of work to a national treasure."

Doherty pulled back, taking another look at the proposal. "National treasure?"

Colin glanced to Shannon. She seemed irritated, but also desperate. Colin smiled reassuringly at her, then went on. "What you will find contained within the pages of that proposal is a comprehensive business plan to brew and supply not only your pubs, but half of the rest of the pubs in Ireland, provided the actual brewing operations can be scaled up enough. What you will find is figures detailing the cost of increased production weighed against projections of income. You will find a plan for marketing and advertising O'Shea's Beer as well. In short, sir, you will find everything you need to make Doherty's Pub a name that every Irishman knows and trusts, and the first establishment they will think to patronize when they're looking for a night of fun and companionship."

Perhaps it was a little too enthusiastic, but it seemed to do the trick. Doherty opened the proposal and scanned the first page. His brow shot up in surprise at what he found contained in the pages. Better still, instead of making another excuse or telling him and Shannon off, he kept reading.

"I can assure you, Mr. Doherty, that every question you might have about the scope and vision of this potential partnership is answered in those pages," Shannon said. "No details have been left out. You will even find a page of endorsements at the back from local pub owners in Ballymena who attest to the quality and popularity of my beer above others. I am offering you the opportunity to go into business with me in early days."

"You'll regret it if you don't," Colin added.

Doherty glanced up from reading, looking first at Colin, then at Shannon. "And you say the two of you are in business together?"

Colin glanced to Shannon, making a point of visually deferring to her.

"Yes, we are," Shannon said, though her cheeks went bright pink as she said it. Colin hoped it was because she had suddenly realized what a perfect pair they made and not because she was a terrible liar.

Doherty made a sound that could have been approval —or perhaps was just a huff—and nodded. "I'll read through this thoroughly," he said, holding up the proposal. "You've given me quite a bit to think about. I won't be able to make a final decision until after Christmas, though. Could we set up another meeting before New Year's?"

It was the victory that Colin had hoped he would be able to help win for Shannon. She and Doherty came up with a time to meet between Christmas and New Year's, the three of them shook hands, and Doherty showed them back downstairs. He offered them lunch, but Shannon declined, and moments later, they were out on the street, basking in the sunlight and triumph.

"You did it," Colin said, grasping Shannon's arms, wanting more than anything to drag her into his embrace, hug her, and never let her go.

"I dare say that you did it for me," she said, more than a little stunned. "He would have turned me away, just like the others, if not for you."

"But he didn't," Colin said. "And this calls for a celebration." He grabbed her hand and started down the road, then across the street with her, turning more than a few scandalized heads as he did. "I wish you'd accepted Doherty's offer for lunch, because I'm starving. But we can remedy that."

"I believe I saw a tea house on the other corner," Shannon said, glancing over her shoulder.

"That most certainly will not do," Colin said.

He sought out the biggest, noisiest pub he could find at midday in the middle of the week, dragging Shannon through its doors. The lunch crowd inside was larger than he would have expected, but that might have had something to do with the small band of musicians playing merrily away on a small dais at the far end of the front room.

"Brilliant," Colin said. "We can do more than just celebrate—we can dance."

"We will do no such thing," Shannon protested. Her eyes were wide as she glanced around the room at the laughing, shouting, gawping patrons.

Colin ignored her with a mischievous grin, tugging her closer to the bar. "Two pints," he called out, reaching into his coat with his free hand to grab his wallet.

"Sorry, sir, we don't serve women here," the bartender said. He quickly changed his tune, eyes popping wide, when Colin flashed a five-pound note at him. "Coming right up, sir," the bartender laughed, then turned to pull them two pints.

"Colin, we cannot do this," Shannon insisted, though when Colin removed his coat, she unbuttoned and shrugged out of hers as well. More than that, she had a flash of naughtiness in her eyes, even as she said, "They are not allowed to serve me here. They'll call the police. We'll be dragged off to prison, and I will be branded a fallen woman."

"I think you would enjoy being branded a fallen woman," Colin said, taking the pints that the bartender handed them over. He passed one to Shannon. "In fact, I think you would thrive as a fallen woman, especially if I fell with you."

"I would not," she protested, but just like her protests earlier, Colin could tell it was all for show and on principle.

He took a long swig of his beer, then another,

watching and waiting for Shannon to do the same. She sent him a scathing look, then glanced around worriedly, then finally decided to take the plunge and sipped at her beer. That sip turned into a longer drink, and her eyes narrowed in thought.

"It's not as good as mine," she said, "but there's something memorable about it." She took another long drink, then asked the bartender, "What brand is this?"

The bartender didn't have a quick answer. Even if he had one, it would have been too late. Colin finished his pint, then slammed the glass on the table. "Drink up," he told Shannon, tipping up the base of her pint glass to make her drink more, then pulling the glass away from her and putting it on the bar, even though she'd barely finished a third of it.

Shannon blinked in surprise, then wiped her mouth with her gloved hand. That was all she had time to do before Colin grabbed her hand and whirled her out to the floor in front of the band to dance.

"Stop it at once," she ordered Colin as he slipped his arm around her and bounced into a lively jig with her. "It is the middle of the afternoon. I am not dressed to dance in a pub."

"Take a bit more of your lovely clothes off and you will be," Colin told her with a broad smile, whirling her around the floor in front of the band.

Shannon yelped in offense, which Colin was willing to admit he deserved, and glowered at him. That was no deterrent for Colin, though. He kept on dancing, spinning and twirling her, but mostly holding her in his arms, as the pub's patrons clapped and encouraged them.

It couldn't last, as much as Colin might have wanted it to. A well-paid bartender and a bunch of inebriated patrons weren't enough to stop the pub's rules against women being enforced.

"Get out of here, and take your strumpet with you," a broad-shouldered man boomed at them as he strode in from the back room. "I don't allow funny business in my pub."

Perhaps it was the pint of beer he'd downed in a hurry, or perhaps it was simply the joy of having a triumphant Shannon in his arms, but Colin's head spun with joy, even though the pub owner gathered up their coats and Shannon's satchel, marched them over to the door, and more or less manhandled Colin and Shannon back out into the street. Colin considered it a stroke of luck that the pub owner made certain they were thrown out with their things, but they were most certainly thrown out.

"I have never been so humiliated in my life," Shannon insisted as she hurriedly put her coat back on, looped her satchel over her shoulder, and stormed up the street toward the mews where her wagon was parked.

"That wasn't humiliating, that was exhilarating," Colin insisted, following her like an overexcited puppy. "Let's get ourselves thrown out of another pub."

He tried to tug Shannon into a second establishment, but she was firmly against it.

"Thank you for your help today, Colin, but we've accomplished what we've come here for, and I, for one, would like to return home," she said.

"But would you? Truly?" Colin asked as they reached her wagon, which was ready to go.

"Yes," Shannon said.

Colin managed to trap her with her back against the side of the wagon. He knew he was being reckless, but as far as he was concerned, Shannon was the most wonderful woman on the earth, and he would give anything he had to spend the rest of his life with her.

"Let's run away," he said, sweeping her into his arms and holding her close. "Let's set out for China, or America, or Brazil. Let's take your beer recipes and build a whole new empire for ourselves, just you and I."

"You cannot be drunk so quickly," Shannon said, gripping his arms as though she might try to extract herself from his embrace, but also staying right where she was. "You only had one pint."

"I am drunk on you, my beautiful, marvelous Shannon," Colin said, feeling ridiculous and alive. "You were magnificent in there. You are the most intelligent, most determined woman I have ever met, and all I want to do is lay myself at your feet and worship at the altar of your brilliance."

"Well, now we know," she said in a surprisingly matter-of-fact way. "You cannot hold your drink."

"I am not drunk," Colin said truthfully, "and I'll prove it to you."

He leaned in, slanting his mouth over Shannon's and kissing her with all the wild passion he felt. She was surprised at first, but as quickly as he knew she would, she softened into his embrace, humming with pleasure as his lips molded to hers. He parted her lips and slipped his tongue against hers, tasting beer and sweetness. One kiss, and he would never be able to get enough of her.

For a few, glorious seconds, Shannon softened against him, kissing him back. Then she jolted, as if suddenly aware of what she was doing. She pulled away, gasping, and met his eyes with a look of fire.

"How dare you?" she yelped, her entire countenance sparkling with arousal and delight.

Colin was certain she would slap him across the face, and equally certain he would have liked it, particularly as he knew he deserved it. Instead, she wriggled away from him and clambered up onto the wagon's seat. She grabbed the reins and held them taut, staring down at him with her kiss-reddened lips.

"For that, you can find your own way home, Lord Stamford," she said before slapping the reins and propelling the wagon forward.

Colin leapt back to avoid having his toes squashed and laughed as he watched Shannon drive the wagon out of the mews. She might have been abandoning him in Belfast, but of one thing he was certain: Shannon O'Shea wanted him.

CHAPTER 5

She'd left Colin in Belfast, alone and half drunk. That was the first thought to crack through Shannon's mind like lightning when she awoke the next morning. The man was a fool and a rascal, but he didn't deserve to be abandoned in a foreign city, without friends, without help, without—

Shannon stopped her thoughts with a frustrated sigh and threw aside her bedcovers to climb out of bed. The whelp was far from helpless. He was well-traveled, and if the five pound note he'd plunked down at the bar of the pub he'd dragged her to was any indication, he'd had the cash to hire a carriage to take him back to Kilrea Manor. After the way he'd behaved toward her, he deserved what he got.

The way he'd behaved toward her.

Shannon sighed and leaned against the wall beside her washstand, touching her fingers to her lips. Colin

Crenshaw, the Earl of Stamford, had kissed her. In broad daylight. As easy as you please. And what a magnificent kiss it had been at that. She couldn't stop a smile from forming under her fingertips at the memory. She clasped her free arm around her waist, remembering what his arms had felt like around her. For a young, arrogant lordling, he had powerful arms, but also a tenderness she wouldn't have expected. His kiss had been soft and demanding at once, drawing her in and spinning her head. The feel of his strong, masculine body against hers had been like a glimpse into heaven. The imp had bragged about being a good lover, but after that kiss, that embrace, Shannon believed him.

She was no fainting violet, no innocent maiden without knowledge of the ways of the world. She was considered a spinster in some circles and a hoyden in others for her unconventional ways. Almost no one knew the full details of her brewing business, but they knew she had no interest in garden parties and husband hunting. It wouldn't be so terribly shocking if she were to indulge in Colin's skills, if given half a chance. It wasn't as though she had a line of suitors waiting to ask for her hand, or much of a reputation to protect. If things continued on the way they were between the two of them, would it really be so wicked of her to consider surrendering her virtue to the scamp?

Her hand started to wander as she considered the question, reaching up for her breast under the thin layer of her nightgown, then making a circle and heading down. Would it really be so much of a sin if she were to find herself secluded somewhere with Colin, trapped in his embrace again? Her hand traveled lower still. Perhaps she could apologize for leaving him in Belfast in the most intimate of ways. If they happened to find themselves—

Her door flew open and Chloe burst in with, "Shannon, you must help me decide which dress to wear to today's luncheon. I'm playing hostess for the first time, and—oh!"

Chloe's expression slipped into a teasing grin as Shannon jerked her hand away from where it had been heading and flinched so hard against the wall that she nearly knocked herself over. Her face and neck heated viciously, and she was certain the very guiltiest of looks graced her face. And blast it, if she'd just stayed calm and pretended nothing was out of the ordinary, Chloe never would have had a reason to wear that knowing smirk that tugged at the corner of her mouth now.

"And how was your day with Lord Stamford yesterday?" Chloe asked, swaying toward Shannon as if she were in on the secret.

"It was fine," Shannon squeaked, crossing to her wardrobe to select an appropriate gown for the day. She'd forgotten that the entire wedding party, Cousin Caelian, and a few close friends would be having lunch at Dunegard Castle that afternoon. It meant she would come face to face with Colin again.

Colin, whom she still couldn't stop thinking about. Whose kiss she could still feel on her lips and whose arms she wanted desperately to hold her again. Colin, who she'd dumped in Belfast because the intensity of her feelings toward him had startled her.

"You cannot do wrong if you wear your Belgian lace," Shannon said without looking at Chloe as she picked through the dresses in her wardrobe. "It is fine enough for a semi-formal occasion, such as the luncheon, but not so formal as to be the sort of thing one wears to a ball."

"And what will you be wearing?" Chloe asked, taking a seat on the side of Shannon's bed and grinning at her. "Does Colin have a favorite color? Blue, perhaps?" she asked just as Shannon began to pull a blue, muslin gown from the wardrobe.

"I doubt it." She thrust the dress back in with the others and pulled out a green one. "Even if he had a preferred color, I'm sure I wouldn't care."

"Wouldn't you?" Chloe asked. When Shannon turned around, taking her selected gown to the bed, Chloe had one eyebrow raised and a grin that was far too mischievous on her lips.

"No," Shannon said firmly. "I wouldn't."

Chloe hummed and picked at Shannon's coverlet. "Deane told me that Colin returned to Kilrea Manor quite late last night."

"Did he?" Shannon pretended disinterest. She blinked and turned to Chloe to ask, "How was your betrothed able to tell you that his cousin returned late last night when it is barely past nine this morning?"

It was Chloe's turn to flush pink. "I may have been at

Kilrea Manor myself when Colin returned," she confessed.

"Late?" Shannon draped her gown across her bed and assumed a scolding pose.

Chloe let out a breath. "We're marrying in less than a week. Neither of us are particularly inclined to delay"—she made a swirling gesture with her hand—"the rest of it."

"I see," Shannon said, feeling a twinge. That twinge was not jealousy, absolutely not. She was not the least bit jealous of her youngest sister's amorous audacity.

"Colin was in quite a merry mood," Chloe went on, jumping off the bed and moving to help Shannon wash by handing her the sponge. "Even though he found himself abandoned in Belfast yesterday."

Shannon expected herself to huff and frown and complain a bit more about Colin, but the sound she actually made was one of guilt and despair. "I shouldn't have left him like that," she said, rushing through her ablutions as, frankly, the idea of being undressed and touching herself, even with a sponge in a utilitarian manner, was not something she wanted to do in front of her sister just then. "He aggravated me to no end, though," she went on. "He left me no choice."

"You like him," Chloe said in an annoyingly sing-song voice. "You like him very much."

"I do not," Shannon insisted, drying herself off and crossing to her wardrobe to don underthings. "I needed him as a male presence for a business meeting is all."

"Oh, and what was the outcome of that?" Chloe asked, genuinely interested instead of teasing for the moment.

"It went well," Shannon admitted. "Mr. Doherty was willing to consider my proposal." She paused, then added, "Colin proved himself quite useful in that regard."

"He spoke for you?" Chloe asked as she helped Shannon dress.

"He spoke for me," Shannon said, "but not in place of me. He defended me and my ideas, but he did not attempt to pass them off as his own. He supported my efforts without attempting to belittle them."

Shannon sighed and let her arms drop to her sides after pulling her bodice over her shoulders. If she were honest about it all, Colin had behaved like a perfect champion, if not a perfect gentleman. What was more, she had the distinct feeling that he would not forbid her to continue with her business if the two of them were married.

She shook herself and finished with her bodice, and then her skirt. What was she thinking? Just because the whelp had jokingly proposed to her when they'd first met —three days ago—did not mean that he was a viable prospect for marriage. Shannon had no intention of marrying now. She'd waited too long, on the one hand, and she'd found too many other things to occupy her life, on the other.

"Well, I think you look lovely," Chloe said, standing back once Shannon was completely put together—except for her hair, which she would style later. "I think you look just as you should for apologizing to a bright young earl who provided a great deal of help to you and whom you callously abandoned, simply because you are a bit too enamored of him."

"I am not enamored of anyone," Shannon insisted, grabbing a ribbon from her dressing table to tie her hair up in a temporary style. She was certain the heat in her face and her inability to look Chloe in the eye betrayed her, though.

She headed downstairs, dropping Chloe at her room so she could dress, searching for Henrietta, Fergus's wife, to see if there was anything she could do to help prepare for the luncheon. Her restless emotions refused to settle, though. And she still couldn't stop thinking about Colin. Not as she helped Henrietta direct the footmen to bring more dining room chairs out of storage, not as she checked over the hothouse flowers when they were delivered, and not when her niece and nephews were brought down from the nursery to keep Fergus company.

"Shannon, sit down for a moment," Fergus ordered her as he cradled his infant son, Andrew, against his shoulder, rubbing the baby's back. His two-year-old daughter, Eloise, sat on his lap, trying to play with one of the wheels of his wheelchair. "You're as restless and distracted as Ellie here."

"I am not restless, and I am certainly not distracted," Shannon lied. "I am simply anxious on Chloe's behalf.

She wants everything to be perfect for this luncheon, since Henrietta is letting her play hostess."

"The luncheon will take care of itself," Fergus said, shifting his arm from patting the baby to prying Eloise's hand off of the wheel. He glanced Shannon's way with his one eye, eyebrow raised, looking a bit too excited. "This isn't because of a man, is it? I would consider it a fantastic coup if I was able to marry off all four of my wicked, scandalous sisters within a year of returning to Ireland."

Shannon huffed and crossed the room to pluck Eloise out of his chair, hugging her perhaps a bit too tightly. "It is not because of a man. You know I have no intention of falling into the traps you somehow managed to set for my sisters, and—"

Every thought was dashed right out of Shannon's head as she turned to the door of the parlor in time to see Colin striding into the room with a bright smile.

COLIN HAD HARDLY BEEN ABLE TO SLEEP THE NIGHT before, he was anticipating seeing Shannon again so badly. He couldn't wait to see her expression when they came face to face again, to see whether she felt at all contrite about abandoning him, or whether she was just as fiery as ever. He had tossed and turned all night, debating which emotion he wanted to see from her more. When he couldn't decide, he'd lain there, grin on his face, staring up at the ceiling and remembering how beautiful Shannon had been when she was negotiating for her business. And when she was driving on a sunny, Irish morning. And what she might look like during a steamy, Irish summer night, wearing nothing but moonlight and his kisses all over her luscious body. And then he might have pleasured himself mercilessly while imagining it all before finally falling asleep.

But nothing from his imagination was half as wonderful as the sight of Shannon in the parlor of her brother's house, her hair mostly loose down her back, a babe in her arms. Colin had never fancied himself the sort of man who wanted heirs to carry on his name. As far as he was concerned, his name and his title could die with him. But the visceral sense of rightness that struck him at the sight of Shannon holding a baby hit something primal in him.

"Good morning, my darling future bride," he said, striding boldly into the room.

Behind him, Deane muttered, "Oh, Lord," but Colin ignored him. "Lord O'Shea," Deane went on to greet the rather striking man in the wheelchair holding a baby, who had to be Shannon's brother.

"Blackburn, it's good to see you again," Lord O'Shea said. "Forgive me if I don't get up," he added with a teasing look.

Colin liked the man instantly, which was convenient, since he intended to speak to O'Shea about Shannon's hand as soon as the opportunity presented itself. There would be time for all that later, though. At the moment, he only had one thing on his mind.

"I trust you had a pleasant afternoon yesterday," he teased Shannon, sidling up to her and taking up a position by her side, ostensibly so he could make faces at the baby in her arms.

"Not now," Shannon hissed at him, her green eyes sharp with about a dozen emotions.

Colin grinned at her. He'd only just arrived, and already he had her off-balance. He couldn't have asked for anything more perfect.

"Do the two of you know each other?" O'Shea asked, shifting the infant from his shoulder to his arms as the wee thing slept. He sent a look Shannon's way that Colin could only describe as victorious.

"They met when Colin arrived," Deane said, stepping closer to O'Shea. "Fergus, may I present to you my cousin, Lord Colin Crenshaw, Earl of Stamford."

"Try to sound a bit more encouraging when you introduce me to my future brother-in-law, cuz," Colin said, winking at Shannon, then crossing to extend a hand to O'Shea. "And please call me Colin."

O'Shea's brow went up, which was quite a sight, as he only had one eye and an eyepatch that made him look brigandish. He took Colin's hand and shook it, then sent an amused look to Shannon. "Where do you lot find them?" he asked, sounding both incredulous and entertained. "Is there a catalog of daft lords that you and your sisters have been ordering from without my knowledge."

"Fergus," Shannon snapped, her face bright red.

Before Shannon could defend herself further, Lady Chloe skipped into the room. "Oh, you're here!" She went straight to Deane's side, hugging his arm and gazing adoringly up at him. There was a mischievous light in Lady Chloe's eyes as well—something that likely had to do with the reason she was at Kilrea Manor after midnight the night before. "I've just spoken to Marie and Christian in the hall, and they are wondering if we might go straight through to luncheon, since Marie has quite an appetite these days. I believe Colleen and Benedict will be here any moment, so why don't we go through?"

The maids who had been observing from the side of the room came forward to fetch the babies, and the adults shuffled around, making their way out of the parlor and along toward wherever lunch was being served. Colin quickly leapt to Shannon's side, offering his arm.

"This isn't a formal dinner," Shannon told him in a low hiss, walking ahead of him. "Ladies do not need to be escorted in."

"Ah, but ladies as fine as you should always be escorted wherever they go," Colin argued, unable to keep the grin off his face. He couldn't keep his eyes off Shannon's lips either. He wondered how long it would take before she would let him taste them again.

"Lord Stamford, behave yourself," Shannon scolded him as they fell a few steps behind the rest of the party. "This is my brother's house."

"You do know how thrilling I find it when you set me

71

in my place like that," he said, wiggling his eyebrows at her.

He expected another set-down, but the look of temptation that Shannon sent him was ten times better. Yes, she wanted him, all right. It didn't take a lothario to see the interest in her eyes or to interpret the way her body swayed toward him. Some might argue three days was not nearly enough time for love to blossom, but for Colin, that was more than enough.

As soon as they made the turn into the dining room, Shannon straightened, cleared her throat, and put as much distance between the two of them as she could. Which, of course, had the exact opposite effect from what Colin figured she was going for.

"I see that you and Lord Stamford are getting along swimmingly," Lady Kilrea said from where she was already seated at the far end of the table, her husband beside her.

"Yes, I noticed that as well," O'Shea commented, sending Lady Kilrea a knowing look across the table.

"Has Shannon found herself a beau?" an elegant woman whom Colin had yet to meet asked as she helped wheel O'Shea into the spot at the head of the table.

"Lord Stamford, may I introduce my wife, Lady Henrietta O'Shea," O'Shea made the introduction across the length of the dining table. "And yes, I think Shannon has found herself a beau, and I'd wager he's as mad as the rest of them."

Colin nearly snorted with laughter as he followed

Shannon around the table, in spite of her efforts to shake him off, and took the seat next to her. He didn't only love Shannon at first sight, he loved her entire family as well. They were worlds different from the stilted, stuffy Crenshaw family, Deane excluded.

"Who's mad?" another man asked as he strode into the room, a red-headed woman who was obviously an O'Shea sister at his side. A single gentleman—also with red hair and clearly an O'Shea of some sort—came in with them.

"You are, Boleran," O'Shea called from the end of the table. "All of the men my sisters have or are about to marry are mad. Glad you could join us, Caelian," he nodded to the single gentleman.

"I wouldn't miss a family luncheon for the world," Caelian said. "Something always happens that we end up talking about for weeks."

"That is definitely true," the gentleman, Boleran, said with a jovial smile.

"Today, we can talk about the fact that Shannon appears to have ensnared Lord Stamford," Lord Kilrea informed the newcomers.

"Shannon, really?" the woman Colin assumed was Lady Boleran asked with a bright smile.

"No, I have not," Shannon barked like a fishwife as Caelian tried to hide his laughter while finding a seat at the table, "and I will thank the lot of you to keep your gobs shut and let me eat my lunch in peace." She punctuated her statement by spearing a dressed chicken leg from the platter that had already been placed on the table.

Deane was still standing and took it upon himself to make all of the necessary introductions. Colin was completely delighted with the extended O'Shea family. None of them stood on ceremony as the luncheon was served, and every one of them seemed intent on talking over the others. It was as jolly as the country meals he'd enjoyed in the south of France. More than that, the combined O'Shea family gave him hope that not every family of the aristocracy was dull and formal. His parents would probably die of apoplexy if they sat down for a meal with the O'Sheas—which reminded him that in just a few days' time, that scene might have a chance of playing itself out, as his parents were coming over for the wedding. Not until the very last minute, of course, because his father would rather be caught dead than on Irish soil.

He was dragged out of his thoughts, blessedly, as the conversation shifted to Shannon.

"I say it's about time that Shannon found a beau of her own," O'Shea teased her from the head of the table.

"For the last time, I haven't found a beau," Shannon sighed impatiently.

"Oh, but we would all be so happy for you if you had," Lady Kilrea said, sending Shannon a sympathetic look.

No, on second thought, Colin found the look pitying, and it irritated him. In no way did Shannon deserve pity.

But Lord Caelian seemed to be the only one who shared that feeling.

"Yes," Lady Boleran agreed with a too-soft smile. "Shannon has taken care of all of us for so long, it's well past time that she found someone to take care of her."

"Thank you, but I do not need taking care of," Shannon said, her eyes on her plate as she ate.

"She really doesn't," Lord Caelian said, but too quietly to be noted.

"We do worry about you, dear," Lady O'Shea went on with another pitying look. "We only want you to be happy."

"Yes, which is why I am so happy to have you play such a large part in my wedding." Lady Chloe smiled.

Colin felt Shannon tense by his side. He glanced carefully around the table as Shannon's family sent her varying degrees of concerned looks. He could imagine that for the eldest sister of such a large family, to suddenly be the object of that sort of condescending care now must have been grating.

"Perhaps we are joking a bit too much about Lord Stamford," Lady Kilrea said, still smiling at Shannon. "But even if he is not the one, we do hope you find your happiness soon."

Shannon put down her fork and glared at her sisters. "Were we all not, just one year ago, determined to lead independent lives as our own selves and not someone's wife?"

The three other sisters and Lady O'Shea looked sheepishly around at each other.

"Yes, dear, but perhaps we were wrong," Lady Kilrea said. "There is much to recommend a married life."

"And there is much to recommend the life of a woman who follows her own path," Shannon said, though not very loudly.

Colin couldn't stand the censorious looks Shannon was getting for another second. "Lady Shannon is brilliant," he defended her. "She is an accomplished businesswoman and brewer. Why, you should have seen her yesterday in her meeting with Mr. Doherty in Belfast. She handled herself far better than most of the businessmen I know, and she convinced Doherty to seriously consider her proposal for going into business with her and expanding her brewery as well."

Dead silence fell over the table. The O'Shea sisters swapped anxious looks, then glanced to Shannon, then to Lord O'Shea. O'Shea swallowed the bite in his mouth awkwardly, then reached for the glass of water at his place. Shannon was as tense as a tiger by Colin's side. Colin knew beyond a shadow of a doubt that he'd done the wrong thing.

"Shannon," O'Shea said in a gruff voice after he finished with his water. "Have you continued on with that ridiculous brewery business? After I expressly forbid you to continue to engage in it?"

Colin's heart sank to his gut. "She's quite good at it,"

he continued to defend her, though he knew he was prob-ably making everything worse.

Shannon set down her cutlery and moved her hands under the table, though she continued to stare at her plate. Colin could feel her fuming.

"Shannon?" O'Shea demanded again in a louder voice. "Have you disobeyed me in this as well as every-thing else?"

"I am not a child," Shannon shouted, pushing her chair back so fast that it nearly tipped over, and standing. Her hands were balled into fists at her sides. "I am not some ninny who must be ordered about by her brother or a husband. You left us, Fergus. You went away to fight in the Transvaal, and then you lingered in England. We made lives for ourselves after Mama and Papa died. You cannot expect to waltz—or rather roll—back into Dune-gard Castle and push us around, as though we are pieces on a matrimonial chessboard. I am my own woman, and I will not allow you to steal that away from me, like you did with my sisters."

The tension at the table was so thick that not even cannon fire could have dissolved it. Worst of all, as far as Colin was concerned, Shannon couldn't maintain her furious demeanor. Her face crumpled bit by bit until she broke into a sob. She clapped her hand over her face and dashed away from the table, fleeing the room.

"Oh, dear," Lady Chloe whimpered, gazing after Shannon, but staying where she was.

Colin wasn't so cautious.

"Well done," he hissed derisively, standing and throwing his serviette down on his half-finished plate. He glared at O'Shea as he did. "Well done indeed. You've reduced a strong and beautiful woman to tears, all of you." He glanced scoldingly around the table at the others, except Lord Caelian. "Can you not imagine how hard it must be to see all of her sisters married off in such a short time, abandoning her? Can you not see that the solution to that problem is not pushing her away from her family even further by marrying her to a stranger? Or forbidding her from the one endeavor that makes her feel as though she has worth?" He glared straight at Fergus O'Shea. "If you only had half a notion of how brilliant she is and how much she has accomplished on her own you would be begging for her to teach you all of her secrets instead of pitying her, like she is something old and used up." He stepped away from his place. "I was charmed and delighted by the lot of you just fifteen minutes ago, but now I am not certain I wish to know any of you."

"Colin," Deane cautioned him with a scowl.

Colin ignored him. "I'll see myself out," he said, marching for the door.

He found it telling that not a soul in the room said a word as he left.

CHAPTER 6

S hannon couldn't remember the last time she'd been so humiliated, and she'd spent the last several years of her life running around after her unruly sisters as society spurned them. She'd thought that with all the changes and upheavals in her life at least she could count on her family to make her feel as though everything would be all right in the end, but they'd all just belittled and humiliated her beyond recognition. And in front of Colin.

Not that Colin mattered. He was just some frivolous young lordling who had waltzed into her life less than a week before, as silly as you please and—

Shannon let out a sigh as she reached the carriage house, where her bicycle was stored. She was fooling herself if she thought Colin Crenshaw didn't matter. He mattered very much. Because he was the one person who had supported her fully in the last week without casting aspersions on her or trying to force her to be the sort of woman she wasn't.

But, dammit, the whelp was frustrating. She yanked her bicycle out of its place, straddled it in spite of her too-formal skirts, and pedaled out to the drive, then down the slope toward the cottage. Colin had exploded her secret and told Fergus she was still brewing. Her sisters knew, of course. They'd helped her with several batches and with deliveries to local pubs. In a way, it was ridiculous that Fergus hadn't figured out that she was still deeply involved in brewing. But then, in his broken condition, Fergus shied away from going out to pubs or socializing with anyone but close friends and family. She might have felt sorry for her brother for his isolation if he hadn't just been so high-handed with her.

It was Colin's fault for letting the cat out of the bag, though. She was convinced of it, and her temper had returned to towering heights by the time she reached the cottage. Colin Crenshaw needed to mind his own business and go off to play with the other young lordlings who caused more trouble than they should. He needed to leave the grown-ups to their work and stop ruining her life.

She let herself believe that—even though a tiny voice at the back of her head whispered she was merely upset at the way she'd been treated and lashing out at whomever was conveniently on hand—as she dismounted her bicycle and parked it against the side of the house.

Scowling hard enough to dissolve the stones in front of her, she felt along the wall of the house near the back door for the hiding place where the key was kept, found it, and let herself inside.

The cottage was her refuge, and if she'd had her way, it would be her home. The happiness she'd felt during the years she'd spent living there with her sisters was imbued in the walls and woven into the carpets and curtains. The cottage meant freedom for her—and for her sisters as well, though they seemed to have forgotten entirely what it felt like to be free. There was a chill in the house that came from having more unlit fireplaces than lit ones, but she always made certain the stove in the kitchen was kept smoldering in one way or another, and it was a simple thing to feed the firebox to bring the large stove to life.

She moved about the kitchen, lighting a fire in the older fireplace that had been used for cooking before the stove had been installed, then crossed into the main parlor to light the fire there, if only to give the whole house more of a lived-in feeling. Then she returned to the kitchen and did what came most naturally to her—she set to work bringing out her brewing vats and supplies, filled the largest vat with water, and set it over the fire to heat. If Fergus thought he could stop her from brewing and selling her beer, he had another think coming.

She was halfway through measuring ingredients for a simple lager when a knock sounded on the front door. Normally, she wouldn't have minded, but in her current state, the sound had her leaping out of her skin with dread. She heaved a sigh, slammed the cup she was measuring barley with on the large, sturdy kitchen table, then stomped through the house to answer the door.

She shouldn't have been at all surprised to find Colin standing there on the other side. "What do you want?" she demanded, planting one hand on her hip. "Come to enforce Fergus's dictate that I should start doing something useful with my life and become an ornament in a titled husband's house?"

Colin blinked, then said with far more concern than Shannon thought she deserved, "No, I was told by one of the footmen that you might have come here, and I wanted to make certain you are all right."

Shannon's heart tried to melt at the concern, and at the way Colin's soulful blue eyes went soft as he looked at her. The fury she still felt wouldn't let her capitulate to those feelings though.

"Of course, I am all right," she snapped, pivoting and marching back through the house to the kitchen. Colin shut the door and followed her. "Why wouldn't I be anything but blissfully happy with the care and concern my family has shown for me and my unfortunate marital state?"

"They weren't fair to you," Colin said as they stepped into the kitchen.

He was unusually subdued—or at least more subdued than Shannon had ever seen him before. She headed straight back to the table where she had been working, finished measuring barley, and dumped it into the vat of warm water over the fire.

Colin's posture loosened as he gazed around the kitchen, taking the whole thing in. His brow lifted and his eyes were bright with interest as he glanced from the vat over the fire to the second vat sitting in the sink to the stove. The kitchen was littered with various other brewing implements as well.

"You have quite an operation at work here," he said, seemingly impressed.

"This is nothing," Shannon snapped, not ready to let go of her anger yet. "There is a much larger vat and fire pit set up out back that allows me to brew larger batches. Even that is insufficient for what I would truly like do to, though. But I doubt my esteemed brother will allow me to continue negotiations with men like Mr. Doherty to expand the business, now that you have tattled on me."

Colin's eyes went wide, and he jerked away from studying the fermenting vat to stare at Shannon. "How was I to know that your own brother was unaware of your business?" he asked, giving her as much indignation as he was getting.

Knowing that Colin was upset with her felt good in a paradoxical way. Like the fire that turned simple barley and hops into intoxicating beer, it fueled her.

"Of course my brother did not know of my continued business efforts," she nearly shouted. "Do you think an earl would allow his sister to continue on as a brewer if he knew the truth, my lord?" She flung his title at him as though it were an expletive.

Colin's eyes went wider as he moved around the table to stand near her. Shannon busied herself checking the progress of the batch of beer that was fermenting, and another that was ready to be primed and bottled.

"If you were my sister, I would allow you to do whatever you'd like," Colin insisted. "And I would support you in your efforts."

Shannon sent him a humorless laugh over her shoulder. "You say that now, but if you were truly in this sort of situation, you would behave the same as any other man."

"I would not," he insisted.

"You would shackle your womenfolk to their tea sets and their embroidery hoops and force them to become every cliché of the perfect angel in the house that every moralizing pamphlet and improvement society demands a woman be," Shannon growled, crossing past him to check the state of the bottles she needed to sterilize.

"Now who's being high-handed," Colin grumbled, walking with her. "You've decided on my character based on a cliché when you have had more than enough evidence, including my own statements to the fact, that that is not who I am."

"You say that is not who you are, but how do I know you will not simply change your mind and become like every other idle lordling at the first chance you get?" Shannon asked.

Almost before she could finish her question, Colin roared, "Do you know how much I despise that word?"

The passion behind his question was so strong that Shannon flinched and her eyes went wide.

"*Idle*," he spat the word. "I am not some idle rogue who plays cards and goes hunting and chortles over brandy and cigars at my club. Even though that is all anyone expects me to do." He took a step closer to her. "I detest lolling around, lording it over others, and turning up my nose at anyone who—God protect us—*works* for a living. Contrary to what you evidently think of me and my sort, earls do not merely wish to have fun and make a nuisance of themselves."

A prickly jolt of shame ripped through Shannon at the vehemence in Colin's words. More than that, however, a more exciting, arousing shiver passed through her as well at Colin's seriousness and forcefulness. The power he exuded as he stared at her, so obviously filled with frustration at being trapped in his class and position had her heart thumping against her ribs and her blood pulsing to all the right places.

She couldn't let herself merely capitulate to him, though, so she planted her hands on her hips—to stop herself from throwing her arms around him—and said, "Fine. You do not wish to be idle? You wish to work?" She stomped over to the end of the table and picked up a masher, taking it to him and thrusting it nearly in his face. "The contents of that vat over the fire need to be mashed to create wort. Have at."

Still glaring, Colin swiped the masher from her and crossed the room to the vat. His expression softened for a moment as he stared at the vat, likely working out the best way to do the actual mashing, then he thrust the masher into the vat's soupy contents and ground away.

Shannon stood where she was for a moment, catching her breath and watching Colin. He seemed to have a great deal of frustration that he put into mashing the mixture of barley, yeast, and her proprietary blend of spices that gave her beer just a little kick. Just watching him work calmed her for some reason. She knew what it felt like to put all of her anger and indignation at the ways of the world into labor.

As soon as her breathing calmed, Shannon moved to the sink and set to work filling up a second vat with the proper amount of water. She had no need to make a small batch of beer, let alone two, but she needed the activity to set her soul to right again. As soon as the vat was properly filled, she moved it to the stove to warm the water, then went to work measuring out the ingredients for her most basic beer recipe.

"How do I know when it's mashed enough?" Colin asked as he stepped away from the fireplace long enough to remove his jacket. He rolled up his sleeves as well, then returned to the vat and his mashing duties. Sweat dotted his brow, which Shannon found particularly enticing, and in his shirtsleeves, she had proof that Colin's arms were as strong as she'd imagined them to be.

"It has to reach a certain consistency," she said,

shaking her cup of barley over the sack to even it out. "Then we add the hops."

"You don't add the hops at the same time as the barley?" Colin asked, not only calmer, but genuinely curious as well.

Shannon shook her head. "I've found that if you wait until everything is mashed first, then add the hops, it gives it a better flavor."

"I see." Colin nodded, staring into the pot.

They continued to work for the better part of half an hour in relative silence. The anger and frustration that they both felt hung in the air for a while before gradually dissipating as well. Shannon showed Colin how to move the vat of wort to the stove and bring the whole thing to a boil before adding the hops, then directed him to move the second vat to the fireplace to mash its contents. In the meantime, she stepped into the dining room to check on the half a dozen small batches of beer that were in the process of fermenting.

By the time they had the second vat fully prepared and boiling away on the stove, filling the kitchen with the scent of beer, both Shannon and Colin had calmed down considerably. They leaned against the table together. Shannon was sweaty, more than a little tired, but strangely content with things. She'd more or less ruined her luncheon clothes, but she wasn't concerned. She had several changes of clothes in her bedroom upstairs, and even though her blouse was ruined, her skirt could probably be salvaged.

"I must look a fright," she said, wiping the back of her hand across her damp forehead and the bits of hair that had escaped and were plastered to the side of her face.

Colin turned to her, so much joy in his eyes that it startled her. "You are the most beautiful woman I've ever seen," he said, his voice deep and full of passion.

On what felt to Shannon like impulse, he pivoted to pin her against the table and swept her into his arms. Before she could even think to protest, he slanted his mouth over hers and treated her to the sultriest kiss she'd ever had. His mouth was warm against hers, and his lips molded to her. That only lasted a moment though before he brushed his tongue against the seam of her lips and coaxed her into opening for him. She did so willingly, eagerly, and let out a moan of pleasure as he slipped his tongue against hers.

Even though there wasn't a drop of alcohol in anything they'd made, Shannon felt her head spin as though she'd drunk an entire batch of her beer. Colin's body felt so good pressed against hers. He had her trapped against the table and she loved it. His arms felt so good around her that she simply had to return the gesture and close her arms around him. Colin groaned with plea-sure as soon as she did, which only encouraged her. She dug her fingertips into his back and arched her body against his, nearly shouting in victory when she felt the hard bulge of his manhood against her belly.

The descent into utter madness happened quickly from that point.

"I want you," Colin panted against her ear as his hands roved her sides. "Say you want me too. Say we can give in to this."

Shannon opened her half-closed eyes fully and looked at him with a mischievous look. "I thought you said you liked it when women ordered you around, not the other way."

"Yes," he groaned, fisting his hands in her skirts. "I love it. Tell me what to do. I am yours completely."

Shannon surged into him, kissing him with a wildness she didn't know she possessed. She couldn't find the words to say what she wanted, though—either because she didn't know what they were or because she was too shy to speak something so wanton and demanding. She showed him with her body instead, wriggling against him desperately.

Colin received the message. He grasped her around the waist and sat her on the edge of the table, then gathered up her skirts so that he could slip between her legs unencumbered. As blissful as it had been to feel his erection against her belly through her clothes, it felt even better to feel it pressed directly against her mound, though the layers of clothes they both wore were still too much. Colin seemed intent on remedying that as he tore through the buttons at the front of her bodice, then expertly unhooked the front of her corset with slightly shaking hands.

It was clumsy and imperfect, but he managed to free her breasts enough to knead them in his hands, easing the ache from being constricted in clothing and replacing it with an entirely different ache that throbbed through her core.

"Beautiful," he murmured before bending down to close his mouth around one of her nipples.

Shannon tipped back, catching herself with her arms and supporting herself at a perfect, sinful angle for him to lavish her breasts with kisses and sucking. She'd never even come close to having a man treat her body that way and was bowled over by how good it felt. Colin pushed her bodice down over her shoulders so that he exposed more of her chest, then grasped and fondled her breasts expertly while suckling one. He had her shivering and moaning with need in no time.

That was bliss in and of itself, but when he slipped a hand under her bunched-up skirts and through the split in her drawers to stroke her aching center, she nearly arched off the table.

"You're so wet," Colin growled, teasing and stroking her and making her breath come in short, shallow pants. "I want to make you come over and over."

Shannon was beyond the powers of speech. All she could do was moan at the sensations he was giving her as he stroked her clitoris, then slipped two fingers inside of her. She wasn't certain her arms would be able to support her under the onslaught of pleasure, and when he dropped to his knees, tugging her hips forward, she was certain she was moments away from flopping back on the table and sending her brewing equipment flying.

She cried out with pleasure as he brought his mouth to her sex and used his tongue to tease and pleasure her. She loved everything about it, even the way he pushed her legs apart wider than they wanted to go. His tongue and mouth were magical on that part of her, and when he added his fingers, reaching inside of her as he licked and sucked her clitoris, she was gone. She moaned wildly as her body convulsed in an orgasm that went on and on as he pleasured her, groaning in carnal delight as he did. It was easily the most glorious sensation she'd ever felt.

She had only just started to come down from it when Colin stood, wiping his glistening mouth with the back of his hand in a gesture that was astoundingly erotic, then fumbled with the fastenings of his trousers. He had them open and had just brought his long, thick cock out—something Shannon wanted to look at and look at until her eyes fell out—when she gasped, "Wait."

For half a second, Colin looked utterly incredulous, as if she'd worked him into a state, taken her pleasure, then planned to deny her.

She would have laughed if she wasn't so overcome with pleasure, and instead said, "Not in the kitchen. I prepare food here."

Colin's expression flashed to a smile and he laughed. "Tell me where, then."

Shannon managed to wrench one arm up and pointed to the hall. "In the parlor. I lit a fire there earlier."

"Good." It was all he said before gathering her against him and lifting her in his arms.

Shannon wrapped her arms and legs around him, her still quivering center rubbing against his freed cock—tantalizingly, but definitely not enough for either of them —as he carried her swiftly out of the kitchen and across the hall to the parlor. He headed straight to a chaise lounge that Shannon had been dead-set against Marie purchasing from a second-hand sale, but which she now saw the genius of, spread her across it so that her legs hung off either side, shoved his trousers down to his thighs, then surged into her so fast and hard that it stole the breath right out of her lungs.

It was wicked, startling, and so amazingly good that Shannon cried out with each of Colin's thrusts. Her body was already sated and over-sensitized, but the feeling of him inside of her, moving with firm, undulating strokes, was bliss. The brief moment of discomfort at being breeched for the first time was utterly forgotten in an instant as she reveled in the sensation of being filled and stretched. It felt natural and perfect, as if her body were meant to accept Colin's. As his thrusts turned faster and harder, along with his breathing and the sounds he made, Shannon bore into it, feeling another orgasm on the horizon and reaching for it.

It was easy to grasp it and let her body explode into pleasure and light again, especially as Colin seemed to have lost control. He growled against her shoulder, then cried out with a final few, deliberate thrusts as a feeling of warmth filled her. Part of her was alarmed that he would spill himself inside of her, knowing what the consequences could be, but the greater part of her didn't care one whit. She loved it, reveled in it, and clasped Colin close as all energy left him and he splayed against her. He felt so right and perfect in her arms, a panting, sweaty mess, that she decided then and there that she wouldn't ever let him go.

CHAPTER 7

olin was in heaven. He'd had no idea that heaven was a seaside cottage on the northern coast of Ireland in mid-December, but he wasn't about to complain. As it turned out, Shannon had her small cottage stocked with more than just brewing ingredients and equipment. The pantry had everything they'd needed to make a simple supper for themselves that night —after finishing with the two batches of beer and securing them to ferment for a few weeks. He'd felt downright domestic as he and Shannon cooked together, ate together, and then retired to her lovely bedroom upstairs for the night—where he had a chance to show her that he hadn't just been bragging when he'd told her how exquisite he was at pleasing a woman in bed. And just as he'd imagined, Shannon was as fiery between the sheets as she was when she lost her temper.

"This is exactly the sort of life I want to live," he

commented the next morning as the two of them lay in bed after a satisfying night of sleep.

"This?" Shannon lifted herself from where she'd been dozing across his chest, her head on his shoulder. The gesture had her thick, ginger hair spilling across her creamy shoulders. There was just enough light coming in through the windows that faced the sea to illuminate her gorgeous, shapely body as the covers slipped down her back.

"Absolutely this," Colin purred, pushing the covers down farther so that he could drink in the sight of her body with a wicked grin.

Shannon laughed, then pulled back and sat up, letting the covers spill completely to the bed. Colin sucked in a breath at the full sight of her nakedness as she knelt between his knees. He also got a thrill at the way she raked his naked body with a lascivious look. He loved how Shannon could go from proper lady to determined businesswoman to sultry siren in the space of just a day. He might have preened a little under her gaze as well, resting his forearms on the pillow above his head and spreading himself out for her pleasure. He couldn't keep the impish grin off his face as he did, especially since he was already getting hard, and Shannon seemed to appreciate it.

"I see you grinning at me like the young fool you are," Shannon told him, one eyebrow raised teasingly. "You're quite proud of yourself for this virile young body of yours, aren't you?"

"Excessively proud," Colin sighed.

His breath hitched as Shannon leaned forward to rake her hands over his chest and sides. She hummed in appreciation as she brushed over him with feather-light strokes, pinching his nipples and making him suck in a breath. That also made him grow harder, which he loved. She had him aching and twitching as she brushed her fingertips down over his hips and along his inner thighs, and he grew so hard that his cock stood up against his belly, begging for more.

"Are you going to let me get away with stroking you like this, my lord?" she asked with a teasing lift of one eyebrow.

"I am indeed," Colin sighed in contentment.

"You're not going to take me in hand, flip me to my back, and have your wicked way with me?" Her green eyes glittered with wantonness.

"No, my lady," he teased her right back. "You're just going to have to have *your* wicked way with *me*." He winked up at her.

"How very unlike an earl," she purred, scooting back so that she could bend forward and kiss his chest, then his stomach, then the tip of his cock as it rested against him.

Colin made a sound of delicious surrender, loving every moment of her teasing. "As I think I've told you," he said, "I do not quite fit the standard description of an earl."

"No, you do not," Shannon said, grinning up at him from the most amazingly tempting position between his legs. "In fact, I'd wager you are a bit too big to fit any mold." She stroked her hand up his cock as she spoke.

Yes, Colin was absolutely in heaven. Where else would a man like him receive a compliment about the size of his prick from a woman as wonderful as Shannon? She didn't just compliment it either. She peeked up at him and flickered her tongue out to taste his head, then made him think he'd died in order to get to the heaven he was in by drawing him into her mouth. It was all he could do to stay still and let her experiment instead of thrusting into her and taking what he wanted. She wasn't able to take much of him, but it hardly mattered, as it was the effort that counted. His breath came in short, desperate pants as she brought him dangerously close to the edge in no time flat.

"Oh, bother it," she gasped after playing with him that way for only a minute or so. "Call me a strumpet if you wish," she continued, climbing up his body until she straddled his hips, "but I need you inside of me."

Colin's breath whooshed out in a heady rush, and he grabbed himself and her hips, guiding her to him so that she could bear down on him. It was the most amazing feeling in the world to feel himself slide deep inside of her wetness as she set the pace and controlled the depth. He loved every second of the way she tested herself—hesitantly at first, then with increasing confidence—as she rode him. It was so perfect and he felt so used—in the very best possible way—as she was taking her pleasure from him, that neither of them lasted particularly long.

They napped again for a short while once they collapsed on the bed together, and when they were rested enough, they got up, washed and dressed. Colin only had his clothes from the day before—which had seen better days—but Shannon had an entire wardrobe of clothes there in the cottage. As far as Colin was concerned, those simple things suited her much better than the finery she'd been dressed in the day before.

Their morning together was perfect. They made and ate breakfast together—Colin considered himself an expert at the art of making tea—then puttered around the kitchen, checking on the beer they'd made the day before, batches that had been fermenting for days or weeks, and preparing bottles to be filled.

"This definitely reminds me of working at the vineyard in France," Colin said as he held the funnel steady so Shannon could pour fermented beer—along with the sugars that would cause it to carbonate—into the bottles they'd readied.

"What possessed you to go to work at a vineyard in France for a summer?" Shannon asked, as casual as could be, as though the two of them worked together like that every day of their lives.

If Colin had his way, they *would* work together like that every day for the rest of their lives.

He shrugged. "I'd finished university, but there wasn't anything for me to truly keep myself occupied after."

"And you aren't the sort of earl who just wants to have fun," Shannon added, winking at him.

She might as well have reached into his chest and seized his heart with that wink.

"Correct," he said, grinning back at her like the enamored schoolboy he was. "I had a university mate whose family was involved in financing the vineyard in question. Something about family ties going back to a debt of gratitude at the end of the Napoleonic Wars. I said I would be interested in working there for the summer, learning the vintner's art."

"I see," she smiled as they moved on to a second set of bottles.

"There was some confusion when I arrived, though," he went on. "A language barrier, as my French was only marginal, in spite of years of tutelage, and the vineyard's overseer spoke no English at all. I was mistaken for a laborer instead of a vintner, but I decided not to correct the man."

"He must have had quite a shock when he found out who you really were," Shannon laughed.

"He did," Colin laughed with her. "And so did Monsieur Archambeau, my friend's friend. He thought I'd gone missing for a week before discovering me up to my elbows in dirt as I helped tend the grapevines."

"And you truly enjoyed it?" Shannon asked, giving him a look as though he could have been exaggerating.

"So much," Colin sighed as they finished filling bottles and went back through, capping them all. "There is nothing in this world as satisfying as a hard day's work in which you feel as though you've accomplished something." He paused, then added, "Unless it's something else hard that is employed at the end of the day."

Shannon laughed out loud at his crude joke, which only made him love her more. Within the span of just a few days, she had offered him everything he'd ever wanted, everything he'd ever needed. And he was ready to ask for more.

"You'll help me deliver these to the pubs I've promised them to in Ballymena, won't you?" she asked once they were finished with the bottles. "I've a few kegs stacked up in the back parlor that need to be loaded into the wagon as well."

"My lady, I am now and forever will be yours to order around as you see fit," Colin told her with an exaggerated bow. He peeked up at her with a salacious expression from his bow and added, "And please, please do order me about *excessively*."

Shannon laughed again and turned such a beautiful shade of pink that Colin couldn't resist standing and sweeping her into his arms for a kiss. It was a glorious thing to kiss her laughter into sighs as she wrapped her arms around him. Perhaps they were in a dream world for the moment. There was a large chance that as soon as they set foot outside of the cottage, the world would remind them that everything they were doing went against the ironclad rules of society, but Colin didn't care.

He had what he wanted in that moment, and he would hold onto it for as long as he could.

He waited at the cottage, arranging the kegs and crates of bottles for easy loading as Shannon rode her bicycle back up to Dunegard Castle—which was within sight of the cottage—then drove her wagon back half an hour later. Colin was impressed with her strength as she helped him with the kegs and crates.

"Well, what do you expect?" she asked with a teasing glint in her eyes as she pushed the last crate of bottles into the wagon bed and they closed the tailgate together. "I've been doing this more or less on my own, with the occasional help of my sisters, for several years now."

Her statement both made Colin's estimation of her grow to towering heights and made him sad. "You won't have to do this alone anymore if I have anything to say about it," he promised.

Shannon blushed and looked bashful for a moment, which came close to making Colin laugh. Everything she did made him love her more.

The trip into Ballymena was an educational one. Since their fight the day before and discovering that Shannon had gotten away with running her business without her brother's knowledge for so long, Colin had wondered how she managed to keep the whole thing a secret from the prying eyes of Ballymena society. The answer was that she kept to the back streets and traveled mostly threw mews. She delivered her beer to the backdoors of the pubs she did business with and accepted cash payments on the spot. It was all extremely clever of her, but Colin could see why she wanted to expand into a more legitimate business.

Best of all, as they made their deliveries, Colin got to play the role of delivery boy. Whenever Shannon ordered him to bring her a keg for one pub or the crates of bottles for another, he said, "Yes, ma'am" and touched the brim of his cap as he scurried to do his bidding. The act was ridiculously arousing to him. He knew plenty of couples played roles with each other when they were being amorous, but he had a feeling that he and Shannon could take those sorts of games to fascinating new heights.

All good things had to come to an end, though, and after purchasing lunch from a vendor in Ballymena and eating it in the empty wagon bed, their legs swinging over the back of the wagon as though they were children, they had to return the wagon to Dunegard Castle, and thus return themselves to reality.

"I have neglected my sister during a very important week of her life," Shannon sighed as they stepped away from the stableman who had come to take the wagon from her once they were back at Dunegard Castle. "I cannot continue to stay away from her."

Colin hummed in understanding. "And I'm afraid I need to make a sincere apology to your brother," he added as they walked toward the house together.

For a moment, Shannon looked alarmed. "You aren't going to"—she hesitated, then swallowed—"apologize for ruining his sister, are you?"

"Heavens, no!" Colin laughed. He felt his face heat as he said, "I may have told your entire family off after you fled the luncheon yesterday."

Shannon's eyes grew and brightened at his confession. "You didn't."

"I did." Colin hung his head sheepishly as they were let into the house through a side door. "And I truly do owe it to the man to apologize."

"Perhaps not." Shannon tilted her chin up, grinning. "Chances are that Fergus deserved it."

Colin laughed rather than telling her he agreed with her.

"I should really go upstairs and change," Shannon began.

They were passing a parlor that looked as though it wasn't used often, and before she could finish her statement, Colin whisked her inside and drew her into an amorous embrace. He slanted his mouth over hers and kissed her with all the passion and happiness in his heart, regardless of how risky it was to do so in her house. He didn't care. He'd found exactly the place that he wanted to be for the rest of his life, and he wasn't going to let anything get in the way of that.

"And I thought *I* was a strumpet," Shannon gasped, smacking his shoulder when he let her go.

"I'm your strumpet," Colin growled.

He swayed toward her for another kiss, but a passing maid put an end to that. The maid didn't see them, but she was a reminder that they were in a position to be caught.

They left the parlor and Shannon brought him to the study where her brother spent his afternoons before continuing on to go about her own business. O'Shea glanced up from the ledgers he was working with behind a desk in time to see Shannon deposit Colin there.

"I suppose I shouldn't be surprised to find you with my sister," O'Shea said without an introduction. He wheeled himself out from behind his desk and faced Colin with an amused grin rather than the stern frown Colin expected. "Would you care to explain yourself?"

Colin opened his mouth to issue his planned apology, but instead he ended up asking, "I'd like your permission to ask your sister to marry me."

He snapped his mouth shut once the question was out. He was certain that he looked far more surprised than O'Shea did.

"I knew it," O'Shea said, shaking his head. "Shannon can fuss and complain all she wants, but she's as inclined to marry as any woman."

Colin's apologetic, hopeful mien dropped to a scowl. "I'll thank you to stop disparaging your sister by underestimating her," he said. "I am asking for your permission not because she is eager to marry, but because I adore her and cannot imagine my life going forward without her. I have yet to even broach the subject with her. Well, other than proposing to her moments after we met."

That seemed to surprise O'Shea somewhat. "She didn't put you up to this?"

"No! Not at all." Colin huffed an impatient breath. "I wish you lot could see what I see when I look at Shannon. She's not some prize to be won by a man with a title. She's a brilliant, industrious woman with dreams and ideas."

O'Shea narrowed his one eye. "And do you plan to let her continue with her brewing business once you are married?"

Colin narrowed his eyes as well. "If I say yes, I absolutely do intend to encourage her efforts, will you deny me her hand in marriage?"

O'Shea surprised him by letting out a breath, dropping his shoulders, and smiling. "Certainly not. Shannon always has needed something to keep her busy. My only concern with her continuing her brewery is that it would prevent her from seeing the sort of happiness that I have found, and that her sisters have found in marriage."

Colin blinked at the man. "So you are not opposed to her business in principle, only because you think it would have stopped her from finding another sort of happiness?"

"Precisely," O'Shea said with a nod. "And if you love my sister and are willing to let her continue with the entire operation, then I give you my blessing." He shrugged as though it were a matter of course.

"Truly?" Colin burst into a smile, his heart feeling light. "You will truly let me ask her to marry me?"

"I will," O'Shea said. "But ask yourself this first." He shifted in his chair, winced a bit, and went on. "You are very young, Stamford. Years younger than my sister. Is this truly what you wish for your life at your age? Are you certain this isn't just some flight of fancy, born of youth and novelty?"

Colin frowned all over again. "If you think that my age has caused me to fall in love without understanding of what that truly means, for my heart or my life, then you do me a grave disrespect, my lord. I have lived more than most young men in my position, and I wish to continue to live a full life, not one of idleness and sloth. Your sister is the only woman I have ever met who has been willing to support me in those endeavors, which is why I want nothing more to support her in hers."

Silence rang through the room as Colin finished.

Slowly, O'Shea smiled. "Then you truly are the right man for Shannon," he said. His smile broadened. "And I get to crow about matching up every one of my sisters within a year of returning to Ireland." He chuckled. "I will give those matchmaking ninnies of high society a run for their money after all. Perhaps I should begin charging for my services."

Colin laughed along with him, even though he wasn't certain he should. Perhaps he could come to be friends with Lord O'Shea, and the entire O'Shea family, after all.

"Then, if you will excuse me, my lord," he said, giving O'Shea a short bow, "my parents will be coming over for my cousin's wedding in just two days, and if I send a telegram immediately, my mother may be able to bring over an heirloom ring so that I can make my proposal to Shannon properly."

"Then by all means, go," O'Shea said, making a shooing gesture. "There is a telegraph office at the post office in Ballymena. They will probably still be open if you hurry."

"Then hurry I will," Colin said, turning and running out of the room. He headed back through the house, intending to go to the carriage house, where Shannon said she kept her bicycle. He didn't think she'd mind if he borrowed it without asking, particularly considering the errand he needed to use it for. And if all went well, the two of them would be engaged as soon as his parents set foot on Irish soil.

CHAPTER 8

*I*t was a small bit of a blow to Shannon's pride that a man could sweep into her life and change everything when she'd worked so hard to set herself up as an independent woman of business. She couldn't help but feel hypocritical in several ways for having her head turned when just a few days ago, she had lamented to Colin about her sisters falling prey to the marriage trap. She wasn't certain she truly wanted to marry Colin. She wasn't certain he truly wanted to marry her. He had only asked her in jest, after all, before everything had blossomed between them. A wicked part of her relished the idea of simply living in sin with him in the cottage, building her brewery business together, and being thoroughly shunned by "good" society.

It wasn't something she had to put her thoughts to immediately, though. Chloe's wedding needed to take first priority in her mind. It was only a few days away, and there was still much to be done. As it turned out, there were even more things to be done before that, as Colin's birthday happened to coincide with the day his parents arrived in Ireland for the wedding. As Kilrea Manor was busy being decorated for the wedding, Fergus had offered to host a welcoming party for Lord and Lady Wallingsford that would also serve as a birthday party for Colin.

"How splendid to have a beau who is a Sagittarius," Chloe squealed with delight as she and Shannon headed downstairs to the conservatory, where it seemed half of County Antrim was gathered to welcome the marquess and his wife. And if Shannon knew the meddling mamas of the county at all, to inquire after the marital status of Lord Wallingsford's heir. "Particularly as you are an Aries," Chloe went on, even though Shannon rolled her eyes. "No, I mean it," Chloe protested. "I cannot think of two sun signs who are more compatible than Sagittarius and Aries."

"You cannot fool me, Clo," Shannon told her, tilting her chin up as they walked down the last flight of stairs and started across the hall. "All of these astrological leanings of yours are merely an excuse to play matchmaker, and I am not interested," she lied.

Shannon caught sight of herself in one of the hall mirrors as they walked toward the music and chatter wafting from the far end of the hall and smiled. She'd outdone herself, donning one of her favorite gowns—an expensive blue confection that she'd purchased with early profits from her business—and pinning sapphires in her fashionable hairstyle. The blue gems stood out magnificently against the flame of her hair. Colin would be breathless.

Not that she'd dressed to please Colin. Not at all.

"In the first place," Chloe told her with a sly grin, "it is the stars who play matchmaker, not I. I was not the one who wrote the rules of the heavens."

Shannon sent her sister a flat look and hummed doubtfully.

"In the second place," Chloe's grin grew as they neared the conservatory, "you are so interested."

"Blasphemy!" Shannon gasped playfully. "For you know that I have sworn to dedicate my life to my business and to make a name for myself as a brewer."

It was Chloe's turn to stare disbelievingly at her and to tut, shaking her head. "You may be independent, but you are not immune to love."

Shannon had the horrible, wonderful feeling her sister was right as they stepped into the moderately crowded conservatory and her eyes flew straight across the room to Colin. Her heart seemed to skip in her chest, and she wondered if she'd laced her corset too tight. Colin was deliciously handsome in his formal suit, his hair combed rakishly to one side in defiance of the current male fashion for too much pomade and center parts that Shannon abhorred. His suit accentuated his broad shoulders and trim waist, and now that she had direct experience of the body that lay underneath his fine clothes, she allowed herself to see the strong lines of his thighs and the impressive curve of his backside under his trousers. A shiver passed through her, and she wondered when they'd be able to steal away for more naughty activities again.

As soon as Colin glanced across the room and noticed her arrival, his whole face lit with excitement and affection. He said something to the dour, older gentleman and rail-thin, stiff woman with him, then peeled away from them and crossed the room to Shannon with eager strides.

"You must excuse me," Chloe told Shannon with an impish sparkle in her eyes as Colin headed toward them. "I need to be by my groom's side for the evening, and something tells me you want to be by your groom's side as well."

"He is not my—" Shannon huffed a breath through her nose, unable to finish defending herself, as Chloe stole away and Colin rushed in to take her place.

"You look absolutely stunning tonight," Colin said, raking her with a lascivious glance that was entirely inappropriate for a public gathering.

"Put your eyes back in your head, if you please, Lord Stamford," Shannon scolded him in a whisper.

"I'll pluck them out and put them wherever you want them, if you just tell me to," Colin replied, leaning closer to her.

Heat infused Shannon's body, and she tried to fight off the surge of power that she felt every time he made that sort of borderline lewd statement. To ward off her need to drag him out of the room and upstairs to her bedroom, she cleared her throat and said, "Is that couple staring at us from the other end of the room, the gentlemen and lady you were just speaking to, your parents?"

Colin glanced over his shoulder to find that they were still being watched. He sighed, taking Shannon's hands, and said, "They are. And I apologize with my whole heart in advance."

"Oh dear." Shannon sent him a dire look. "Are they the sort of parents that one has to apologize for?"

Colin pinched his face slightly and said, "We do not get along. As Deane likes to say when he's being kind, we come from different generations. Their idea of what an earl should be and mine are very different."

"I see." Shannon nodded. She then tilted her chin up. "Well, as the daughter of an earl myself, and as an experienced woman of the world, I believe that I am up to the challenge of making a good impression on them."

"I believe you are," Colin said with a proud grin, pivoting and offering Shannon his arm.

She took it, feeling everything from dread to triumph as Colin escorted her across the room to make the introductions.

"Mother, Father, I would like you to meet Lady Shannon O'Shea." Colin presented her with more formality than she would have expected from a mischievous whelp like him.

"How do you do Lord Wallingsford?" She dipped into a curtsy for the man, then another for his wife. "Lady Wallingsford."

Whatever Shannon expected, it was not for Lord Wallingsford to roll his eyes, nor for Lady Wallingsford to lift a small lorgnette to her eyes to study her.

"Oh dear," Lady Wallingsford said in a voice of doom. She lowered her lorgnette and frowned at Colin. "She's positively ancient, Stamford. Which back shelf did you pull her off of?"

Shannon's heart dropped to her feet, and her body ran hot and cold. The insult was one thing, but the fact that Colin's own mother had addressed him by his title in such cold tones twisted Shannon's stomach in knots.

"I am but thirty, my lady," she told Lady Wallingsford in a measured voice.

Lady Wallingsford's eyes popped wide. "An impertinent spinster?" She turned to Colin. "Is this the woman to whom you wish to attach yourself?"

To his credit, Colin handled his parents' frosty manners with aplomb. "Lady Shannon is the very best of women, Mother," he said, smiling at Shannon, in reassurance if nothing else. "She is lively and industrious, and I consider her the finest beauty I have ever known."

"She is passingly comely," Lord Wallingsford said, clasping his hands behind his back and staring at Shannon in a way that implied he thought she was anything but. "For someone with that sort of coloring."

Shannon could have easily withered under the man's

scrutiny, but she was determined to hold her own. "Beauty is in the eye of the beholder, my lord," she said, inclining her head to him. "Or so the sages say. But I have many other qualities that define me as well, a head for business being one of them."

She might as well have said that she had cloven feet, judging by the reaction Colin's parents gave her.

"A woman with a head for business?" Lord Wallingsford snorted. "It is not possible. The female brain has been scientifically proven to be too weak for things such as business or education. Any attempts to countermand this fact of nature result in direct harm to the woman's reproductive capabilities."

Shannon's face went hot. Even more so when Lady Wallingsford said, "Are you entirely certain you are still within your child-bearing years, my dear? The Wallingsford line needs an heir, after all."

It took everything Shannon had not to scream in frustration and tell Colin's parents exactly what she thought of them. "I am thirty," she repeated in hoarse clipped tones.

Lord Wallingsford humphed. "Not old enough to have learned how to address your betters, I see."

Shannon gaped. The man was only a marquess. She was an earl's daughter. There was not enough of a gap in their positions for him to address her as though she were the scullery maid.

"Perhaps an example of Lady Shannon's prowess would be in order," Colin said, stepping in with an anxious look. His face had also gone red. "We'll just fetch it for you."

He grabbed Shannon's elbow and marched her away from his parents, all the way across the conservatory to the hall. More than a few of the guests stopped their conversations and turned their heads to see what was going on.

"I know they are your parents, Colin," Shannon said as they turned the corner and headed toward the back of the house, "but they are horrid."

"Yes, they are," Colin agreed, his eyes round. "And I am so, so sorry for the way they raked you over the coals so unnecessarily like that."

"Those were not just coals," Shannon said with a humorless laugh, "those were coals mixed with nettles."

Colin surprised her then by taking her hand and pulling her into a side parlor. He swept her around to press her back against the wall beside the doorway, rested his hands on the sides of her face, and slanted his mouth over hers for a long, tender kiss. The tension that had built in her body over the insults that had been inflicted on her drained away, and she sighed.

"There," Colin said once she was relaxed again. "All better?"

Shannon raised one eyebrow. "You ask that as though I am a child whose hurts you have just soothed."

Colin laughed and stole another kiss before saying. "You are no child. You are a dried-up spinster I found on some dusty, Irish shelf."

Shannon gaped at him in offense as her heart sang in her chest and swatted him playfully. "You are as bad as your mother."

"I couldn't begin to be as bad as my mother," he said seriously, then broke into a smile again as he grabbed her hand. "Now come along. Didn't you say you planned to have some of your beer on hand to serve as a birthday gift to me?"

"I did," Shannon replied cautiously as he took her back out into the hall.

"Then where is it?" Colin paused and looked around, as though a keg would drop out of one of the hall closets. "We'll serve a pint to my father, and when he tastes how wonderful it is, we'll surprise him with the knowledge that you are the brewer."

"No, Colin, I don't think so." Shannon tugged on his hand to hold him back as he tried to move on toward the corridor at the end of the hall that led to the kitchen stairs. "Beer is not the way to win your father."

"Of course it is," Colin insisted, pulling her on. "I know my father better than you do. And beer is the way to win over anyone."

Shannon pursed her lips and let him lead her, though part of her rankled. He might have known his father well, but Shannon knew men like Lord Wallingsford. And when did Colin suddenly get it into his head that he could lead her around as though she were a puppy on a leash? She was meant to be doing that with him.

She put her irritation out of her head and stepped

ahead of Colin, showing him down to the servants' hall, where two kegs of her beer had been brought up to serve the party guests. One of those kegs had already been tapped, and it was a quick and easy thing to pour a pint to take upstairs.

Shannon still thought the whole thing was a terrible idea, but as they reentered the conservatory, Colin carrying the pint, sipping it once to keep it from spilling, Lord and Lady Wallingsford were speaking with Fergus and Henrietta. Shannon was more inclined to let them all speak than to interrupt with beer, but Colin was determined, and as ill-advised as she thought his enthusiasm was, she couldn't do anything to stop him.

"There you are," Fergus said, glancing from Colin to Shannon. "We were wondering where you'd gone off to. Lord Wallingsford would like to get the speeches over with." When Shannon raised her brow in surprise, Fergus added, "His words, not mine," in a low voice.

"What speeches?" Shannon asked. She glanced to Henrietta, but her sister-in-law merely smiled.

"Here, Father, taste this." Before Shannon could say anything else, Colin thrust the pint of beer at his father.

"What the devil?" Lord Wallingsford made an annoyed face and scowled at Colin. He was forced to take the pint, though, and with a deep curl of his lip, he sniffed it, then took a sip. "Ugh." He thrust the beer back at Colin. "What sort of swill is this?"

Shannon knew better than to be offended by anything the horrible man said, but his censure stung all the same. "That, sir, is my beer," she said with barely controlled calm.

"*Your* beer?" Lady Wallingsford raised her lorgnette to her eyes again.

Fergus chuckled. "My sister fancies herself a brewer." He must have seen the fury in Shannon's eyes, because he rushed on with, "And an excellent brewer she is at that."

"God, no." Lord Wallingsford rolled his eyes. He glared at his son. "I trust you plan to remedy this situation as soon as possible."

"I...er...." Colin's mouth hung open for a moment as he gaped from his father to Shannon to the pint in his hand, then back to Shannon. "I suppose so?"

Lord Wallingsford sniffed. "Then let's get this over with."

Shannon was at a loss, particularly when Henrietta took charge to quiet the room and turn everyone's attention to herself and the Wallingsfords.

"On this happy occasion, Lord Wallingsford would like to say a few words," she said.

Prickles raced down Shannon's back. Something was dreadfully wrong. She felt the same sense of anxiety that she had in her early days of brewing, when she'd fumbled the recipe for a batch and had to wait a week to see if it was a failure or an unexpected success.

"Ladies and gentlemen," Lord Wallingsford began in a loud but dry voice. "I thank you all for coming to celebrate my errant son's birthday," he sent a withering look to Colin, "and the impending marriage of my beloved nephew, the Duke of Blackburn." He smiled across the room at Blackburn in a way Shannon thought was entirely unfair to Colin.

"I do not know why we have been dragged all the way to this godforsaken place for a wedding," Lord Wallingsford continued to growl on, "and I sincerely hope my son will not lower himself to hold his wedding here as well. Though he has already lowered himself considerably in his choice of bride."

Shannon's blood seemed to freeze in her veins. Her whole body went numb, and her eyes widened as she glanced to Colin. The whelp had the nerve to look both pleasantly surprised and far too pleased with himself.

"I suppose this is as good a time as any to announce the impending nuptials of my son, the Earl of Stamford, and this chit, Lady Shannon O—something," Lord Wallingsford went on as though announcing there was a dead rat in the piano. "I've given my consent to the match as the lady in question is so well connected, but one's children do disappoint one so. All the same, I give you my son and his betrothed."

Shannon was so stunned and angry that her whole body shook. Where usually the announcement of an engagement would be met with smiles and applause, Fergus's guests just stood there, gawping at Shannon as though they couldn't believe what had just been said. No, it was worse than that. They stared at her as though they *could* believe everything that had been said, but were shocked that someone would actually speak those sentiments aloud.

It was more than Shannon could bear. "How dare you?" she hissed at Colin, fighting back tears.

Colin's apologetic half-smile vanished completely. "I beg your pardon?"

Shannon's fury rose to towering heights. "A marriage announcement? Without even a proposal? Without consulting me first?"

For a moment, Colin looked confused. Then he sucked in an alarmed breath. "I thought you'd assumed, as I had, that we were meant for each other and that the question would be asked eventually."

"*After* the announcement?" She glared at him.

Colin winced. "I didn't realize he would announce it *now*, but why not? I informed Father of my intentions earlier, and the opportunity for an announcement arose. Is that so very wrong?"

Shannon made a ferocious sound of frustration in response. How could the whelp be such an idiot?

"Oh, good God," Lord Wallingsford said, rolling his eyes. "We're not going to have any trouble with this, are we?"

Shannon balled her fists and glared at the man. "Yes, we are," she growled. She turned her furious gaze on Colin, then vented her rage in a wordless cry, then turned to march out of the conservatory and away from the greatest humiliation she'd ever endured in her life.

CHAPTER 9

*O*nce again, Colin found himself in a position of wanting to tell off an entire family for the way they'd treated Shannon. Only this time, the family was his. Worse still, a frustrated voice at the back of his head whispered that he was as much to blame as his father and mother.

But no, that wasn't true. That couldn't be true. He loved Shannon, and he was merely trying to look out for her. As soon as her skirts swished around the corner of the conservatory door and into the hall, he pivoted to glare at his father.

"What kind of an unforgiveable arse are you?" he snapped, handing the pint of beer he held to an unsuspecting guest who happened to be standing near enough.

His father's eyes went wide. "Stamford! There are ladies present," his father hissed, not even deigning to call him by his given name.

"Yes," Colin growled, "and there would be one more lady present had you not blurted out our marital intentions and insulted Shannon in such a boorish and belittling way."

His father snorted. "Stamford, I do not know what this sudden obsession with the Irish chit is, but she is beneath you."

"She is the daughter of an earl," Colin argued.

"From what sort of a family?" his mother added her salt to the wound of the situation. She whispered, "She's *Irish*."

"I beg your pardon," O'Shea said, wheeling his way into the confrontation. "Is there something wrong with the Irish?"

Given the current political climate, his question was so obvious as to be ridiculous. But Colin's mother seemed more taken aback by O'Shea's wheelchair and his eyepatch than by his shock of red hair and obvious accent.

"Think what you will," Colin's father went on. "You young people and your progressive ideas bore me. Stamford, you know as well as I do that you should be choosing the daughter of a duke to be your bride. You should be choosing an Englishwoman."

"I have chosen Lady Shannon," Colin snapped.

He glared briefly at O'Shea, frustrated that the man hadn't intervened sooner, then marched for the door and into the hall, hands balled into fists at his sides.

Part of him wondered—part of him hoped—that

Shannon would flee back to the cottage so that he could chase her there, as he had the last time he'd had to defend her honor. It was too late for that, though, and she'd been dressed in finery that would never allow her to ride her beloved bicycle. He wasn't certain where else she would go, but landed a bit of luck when he caught her at the bottom of Dunegard Castle's main staircase, leaning against the rail to remove her shoes before charging up the stairs.

"Shannon, wait!" Colin called after her, taking the stairs two at a time as he followed.

"Go away from me, you unforgiveable reprobate," she snapped back over her shoulder, picking up her skirts with her shoes clasped under her arm. "I've no wish to talk to you."

Colin flinched as they reached the hallway where he assumed her bedchamber was located. "I beg your pardon?" he asked, pausing for a moment before striding after her. "Did you not hear me defend you down there? My father was being an arse, and I will not stand for anyone treating you that way."

He had almost caught up with Shannon again when she whipped around to glare at him so fast that one of her sapphire hairpins dislodged from her style. "You betrayed me," she hissed. "You went behind my back and undercut everything that I hold dearest."

Colin's mouth hung open in shock. Shannon raced down the hall, throwing open one of the doors near the end and marching inside.

"I don't understand," he said striding boldly in after her. "I spoke up for you, and earned harsh censure from my father, I might add. Not that I truly care."

Shannon hurled her shoes against the wall near her wardrobe. When she turned back to Colin, she pointed viciously at her door. "Get out. This is my private room. It is wrong for you to be here."

"I—" Colin raised his hands in a gesture of defense and confusion.

"No!" Shannon seemed to change her mind. She marched to the door and slammed it, sealing them inside the room. "You do not get the release of leaving so soon. Not until you are held accountable for your actions."

"What actions, you daft woman?" Colin cried, frustration getting the best of him.

He knew he'd done exactly the wrong thing when Shannon's eyes grew huge and her face flared with heat. "How dare you speak to me in such a manner, you whelp?" she shouted. "In the last few days, you have taken or attempted to take everything from me."

"I have no idea what you're talking about." Colin wanted to pull his hair out, Shannon was being so obtuse. "I have helped you. I have defended you. I thought I was being your champion in all things. You might try showing a little gratitude."

Again, he knew he'd stuffed up the situation entirely when Shannon shrieked. She was standing close enough to her bed to grab one of the pillows and throw it at his head.

"You want gratitude? Is that why you've grabbed my life like a chain and are yanking it every which way?" she shouted.

"Shannon, please!" he snapped, at an utter loss as to what else he could say or do.

"Your father just announced our engagement to a room full of my family and neighbors," she yelped, as though that were a cardinal offense.

"Yes, he did," Colin gaped at her, so lost he felt as though he were drowning. "And he did it in the most egregious possible way and without my permission. I took him to task for it as soon as you left the room."

Shannon balled her fists at her sides and glared at him so hard Colin thought he could actually see her shaking. "When did we become engaged?" she asked, biting off each word as though it were sour.

"We—" Colin's mouth dropped open. He'd asked her brother. He'd wired his father to bring the family ring over. He'd bedded Shannon several times during the most delightful day and night he'd ever spent. He'd proposed in jest the moment they'd met. And he'd completely failed to draw Shannon aside to have an actual conversation about marriage with her, knowing that his father could say something at the party.

Deep shame and aggravation for himself for being so impulsive that he would assume the answer to a question he'd forgotten to ask washed over him. But with it came a sick, pulsing feeling of dread and rejection.

"I thought it was understood," he said in a weak voice,

feeling as though he could hear thunderclouds on the horizon of the storm that was about to break over him and Shannon.

Her glare was as fierce as lightning. "You would dare to *assume* my consent to something as intimate and life-changing as marriage?" Her voice rose an octave she was so angry.

"Yes, well, that was not my finest moment," he mumbled. A moment later, he stood taller and took a step toward her. "But I love you, Shannon. I knew it from the moment I saw you. I love you, and I want to spend the rest of my life with you as yours."

"Why?" she demanded. "So you can run roughshod over me, as you did this evening?"

"I—"

"You did not give me a choice about marriage," she told him, voice raised. "You decided my future without even consulting me, took away my freedom, not only to choose in the moment, but to have a mind and a will of my own for the rest of my life."

"I intended no such thing."

She wasn't appeased at all. "You waltzed in and took over my business dealings. A business that I have worked hard for. I have been engaged in that work for more than a year, long before you came along, but with one crook of your finger, you pulled the whole thing out from under me."

Colin's temper flared to life again. "I enabled you to achieve the goals that you have wanted for so long," he insisted. "You would not have been able to do it without me."

Wrong answer again. Shannon's face pinched with fury. "And now I cannot do it without you," she cried. "You've taken that away from me as well. All that hard work, and it will come to naught if Mr. Doherty believes I am alone in the endeavor."

"Perhaps not," Colin said. When she sent him a withering look, as though she believed him to be stupid, it only set him off. "Perhaps it is not your sex which dissuades these businessmen from dealing with you but your peevish stubbornness." He sent her a hard look of his own, not caring that he was saying the wrong thing now. "You cannot even see when someone is trying to help you. All you see is your precious independence being taken away."

"Stolen, not just taken away," Shannon growled. "Stolen as if you had taken all of the money from my strongbox. And what if our indiscretion of the other day has left me with child?" she demanded, throwing an arm out to the side. "If that is the case, you will have destroyed my life further."

"Children do not destroy lives," Colin argued.

"They do when they are born out of wedlock," she shouted back at him.

"We are to be married." He took an angry step toward her.

Shannon scooted back, holding a finger up to him. "Do not come one step closer to me, Lord Stamford. We are *not* to be married. I have no more wish to marry you than I do to marry a donkey, though at the moment I do not see much of a difference between the two."

Colin jerked back, offended and hurt. Doubly hurt, as his pride stung over the fact that it devastated him so much to feel as though she'd rejected him, as though she didn't love him as much as he loved her.

"Fine," he snapped, wishing to God he felt more like a man than a boy who had just had his hand slapped by his nanny. "If you wish to see it that way, I cannot stop you. But as I see it, I've done nothing but offer you my heart and my help. And yes—" he cut her off when she looked as though she would contradict him and drag the argument on, "—I know how precious your freedom is to you. I know what your business means to you. I can imagine that you feel the very heart of your values is being assailed by my honest love for you. But if you are going to turn into an acid-tongued harpy every time you do not get your way, every time you are asked to compromise, then I don't think I wish to marry you either."

"You cannot—" She took a half step toward him.

"Yes, I can," he cut her off before he was entirely certain he knew what she was going to say. "I can and I will, and that's the end of that." He marched toward her door, putting his hand on the handle. "You see? Two of us can play this game. I wish for my independence too. I wish to have someone help me in the impossible bind I live in, day after day, with my family and their horrendous expectations of me. I thought I had found someone who could understand what it felt like to feel trapped in a situation and who might become a partner to get me out of it. I can see that I was wrong."

He wrenched open the door and stepped into the hall.

"Colin," Shannon called after him, her voice heavy with a dozen different emotions.

Colin was too stung to respond to her. He slammed the door behind him and stormed down the hall. Part of him felt more like a man than he had in his young life, but he despised the feeling. He felt like his father, asserting himself and his dominance as a way to shore himself up. His father was forever belittling the people around him because he knew that he could not stand on his own merit.

He didn't feel good about the things he'd said to Shannon, and he wasn't about to ruin her life further by holding her to an engagement she clearly didn't want. He took a moment on the stairs to compose himself, then continued down, smoothing his hands over his suit jacket then combing his fingers through his hair, and headed back into the conservatory.

The party had continued without him. The small orchestra that had been hired for the evening played a merry tune over in the corner while O'Shea's guests chattered and sampled the refreshments that were being brought around to them. O'Shea himself stood—or rather, sat—in an opposing corner, his family around him. Colin's father and mother stood by themselves near one of the fireplaces, chins tilted up and noses raised, as though not a person in the room were worthy of their company. The conversations in the conservatory hushed for a moment as Colin reentered the room, hinting that he and Shannon had been the topic of a great deal of gossip while he was gone, but Colin didn't care. He cleared his throat, then strode straight across the room to his parents.

"You win," he said without preamble once he got there.

"I beg your pardon?" his father grumbled, looking down his nose at Colin as much as any of the other party guests.

Out of the corner of his eye, Colin noticed O'Shea and his entire family heading toward them. "You will have your way, Father," Colin said. "I no longer have any wish whatsoever to marry Lady Shannon, nor does she have any desire to marry me. You can keep the family ring permanently, as I have no intention of marrying anyone at all now."

"What is the meaning of this?" his mother asked, balking. "You must marry and produce an heir so that the Wallingsford line can continue."

"The Wallingsford line can rot, for all I care," Colin snapped.

"You're not getting out of marrying my sister so easily," O'Shea said as he pushed his chair right into the middle of the discussion. "You made a deal to take the impetuous chit off my hands, and I expect you to stick to it."

Colin's father eyed O'Shea as though he were a bit of spoiled meat that had been dropped a little too close to his shoes for comfort. "I regret to say that I agree with Lord O'Shea," he said, surprising Colin.

"You do?" Colin eyed him warily.

"The announcement has already been made," his father said, glancing around the room. "I will not allow you to make me look like a fool by reneging on it."

Colin could hardly believe what he was hearing. His father wouldn't allow him to end an engagement to a woman he disapproved of, an engagement that had never actually been formed in the first place, because of the slight potential it had to make him look bad?

"If you care so little for my happiness, then I question the bond between us entirely," he growled, glaring at his father.

His father barked a laugh. "Were it not for my absolute certainty about my wife's virtue, I would have doubted the nature of the bond between us myself. From nearly the moment you were born, you have been a gross disappointment to me. I only regret that you do not have a brother to take on the family duties in your stead, as you are an utter failure as a nobleman and a son."

On any other day, the blow would only have been a glancing one. But Shannon had already opened up the wound with her rejection. The sting of his father's words was too much when added to the wounds his heart had already received.

"I see," he said quietly, holding himself to his full height, hands clasped behind his back. "I should have expected no less." He turned to O'Shea. "I am very sorry to have importuned you, my lord. I will show myself out now."

Colin turned to go, striding out of the conservatory with his head held as high as he could. As soon as he was away from the rest of the party guests, his posture failed and his shoulders slumped. He rubbed a hand to his face, feeling numb and wondering where he had gone wrong. He had come to Ireland with the intention of running away from his troubles, but instead, he had brought them all crashing down on himself.

It was not too late to run. He had all of his things with him, so it was well within his capabilities to purchase passage to America so he could start a new life there. He would wait until after the wedding, of course. He owed that much to Deane. America seemed like the best idea for him now, though. There was certainly nothing left for him in Britain or in Ireland.

CHAPTER 10

Shannon hadn't thought it was possible to feel worse than she had when being rejected at every turn by men she wanted to go into business with. As it happened, knowing that she was the one who rejected a man who wanted nothing more than to love her and build a meaningful life with her was so much worse.

"Place those flowers nearer to the altar," Colleen directed Shannon and Marie, as well as several maids from Dunegard Castle and Kilrea Manor, as they decorated the church on the morning of Chloe and Blackburn's wedding. "No, a little more to the left," Colleen went on. "The left, the left, Shannon. Are you even hearing me?"

Shannon shook herself out of her stupor, surprised to find herself standing at the front of the church, near the altar, with a huge vase of flowers in her hands. She blinked, glanced around, and made a questioning, "Hmm?" sound.

Colleen stood at the front of the church—the largest one in Ballymena, since everyone who considered themselves anyone wanted to attend the wedding of a duke—in the aisle between the first rows of pews, directing the decorating operation as though she were a conductor in front of an orchestra. She sighed sympathetically and dropped her shoulders as she looked at Shannon.

"I do wish you would tell us what is wrong," Colleen said, stepping forward to join Shannon and Marie on the chancel.

"It must be Lord Stamford," Marie said in a quiet voice, glancing to Shannon with the sort of pitying look she hated. "He's been in a foul temper these last few days as well."

Shannon had almost forgotten Colin was currently residing with Marie and Christian at Kilrea Manor. His parents had been vocal about staying in a hotel in Belfast, in spite of the distance from Ballymena, so that they could be near the ferry and leave as soon after the wedding as they could.

The news that Colin was out of sorts as well attempted to kindle something in her heart, but Shannon was too overwhelmed to feel it.

Colleen seemed to sense as much. "Here," she said, walking forward and taking the vase Shannon held. She handed it off to one of the maids. "Ellie, would you please see to the rest of the decorations? It's nearly time for the wedding party to be out of sight anyhow."

"Yes, my lady," Ellie said, bobbing a curtsy, then taking the vase farther up the chancel.

"You need to come along with us." Colleen stepped forward to take Shannon's arm and lead her away from the altar and back up the aisle to the back of the church.

Marie took her other arm, and as much as Shannon wanted to shake them off, she didn't have the heart for it.

"This truly isn't necessary," she insisted. "There is nothing wrong with me. I am just tired and overwhelmed with all of the festivities surrounding Chloe's wedding."

"You weren't overwhelmed at my wedding," Colleen said with a sly grin.

"Nor mine," Marie said, equally teasing.

"That is because this is the third wedding this year." Shannon didn't expect her voice to come out as melancholy as it did.

Colleen and Marie exchanged looks around her as they drew Shannon down a hall to the room where Chloe and Henrietta were preparing for the wedding. Something about seeing her youngest sister dressed all in white as Henrietta's lady's maid styled her hair only dug the knife deeper into Shannon's heart. That could have been her, if she hadn't flown into a temper and lashed out at Colin.

It wasn't as though he hadn't deserved her censure. Colin had overstepped his bounds horrifically. He was absolutely in the wrong for surprising her with their engagement. But he hadn't been wrong about the necessity of his help with her business, and she had felt like a perfect heel when he reminded her that he, too, knew the pain of being trapped by birth.

"No, no I will not stand for that," Marie said, whisking Shannon across the room and seating her in a chair that faced the door—which had been left open, perhaps by accident.

"Stand for what?" Shannon asked without any energy.

"For you wilting like all of these wedding flowers will in a few days," Marie said, maneuvering herself into the chair beside Shannon. She shouldn't have been out in public with her pregnancy as advanced as it was, but it was Chloe's wedding, and the O'Shea family had never done things properly.

"I am not wilting," Shannon protested with a scowl. "I am simply vexed is all. I had such grand plans for my brewery business, and they all seem on the verge of collapse."

The other women in the room exchanged glances as though none of them believed a word Shannon said.

"Is it true that Lord Stamford forgot to propose to you before his father announced your engagement?" Chloe asked, glancing at Shannon through the mirror where she sat, unable to turn her head while the lady's maid styled her hair.

"Yes," Shannon growled, finding a bit of vigor after all, even though it was anger. She deflated a moment later. "Unless you count the fact that he proposed to me within minutes of the two of us meeting at the ferry dock in Belfast."

Looking back, Shannon found that whole scene ridiculously charming and so very much like Colin. He was all sunshine and light. Yes, he was young and silly at times, but it was a breath of fresh air. He might grow out of the silliness, but she knew he would always be a diamond glittering in a sea of lumps of coal.

"You love him, Shannon," Henrietta told her, moving to sit on Shannon's other side. "Take it from me, a woman who has been married twice. Love does not wait for the right time or place, or even the right person sometimes. And love does not allow you your freedom once it has you in its grip. But life isn't all about freedom and independence."

Shannon frowned at her sister-in-law. "Thank you, Henrietta, but I have no wish to think kindly on love at the moment."

Henrietta smiled softly in return. "This is what I mean. Love does not wait until you are in the correct frame of mind."

"It truly doesn't," Marie agreed with a laugh. "Worse than that, it has a way of spoiling all of your grand plans."

"You do not need to tell me that twice," Colleen said with a laugh, crossing to take a look at Chloe's hair. "Do you think I wanted to fall in love with Benedict? Absolutely not! That was the last thing I wanted. But I am so glad I did."

"This isn't about me falling in love with Colin," Shannon said, her shoulders slumping. "This is about me abandoning my dreams, abandoning hope for the future of my business."

"I thought Colin supported your brewery," Chloe said, looking via the mirror again. "That is what you told me the other day."

"He does," Shannon began slowly, "but supporting is one thing. Taking it over entirely is another."

"Has he mentioned taking it over?" Henrietta asked.

"No," Shannon answered slowly. "But you did not see the way Mr. Doherty was inclined to only speak to Colin about things that I have put my heart and soul into."

"Would Mr. Doherty have spoken to you at all without him?" Marie asked. "Would any pub or brewery owner?"

"And even if they had," Colleen added, "even if they had agreed to go into business with you, are you certain they wouldn't have cut you out as soon as your business and theirs merged?"

Shannon snapped straighter in indignation at the thought. She hadn't let herself consider it before, but Colleen was, unfortunately, right. That didn't solve the problem, though. Even if she had succeeded with Colin, was that truly success?

The deeper question seeped into her next as she asked herself whether succeeding independently would have mattered if she truly loved Colin, if she could have had him by her side and in her bed for the rest of her life.

"I'm not certain the situation can be salvaged," she said, watching the far end of the hallway through the open door as a few guests began to arrive for the wedding. "Words were spoken."

Marie, Colleen, and Henrietta all scoffed and snorted.

"Words will always be spoken," Marie said sagely. "Christian and I have had one or two shouting matches already. And they have lovely consequences, once the shouting is over," she added with a wiggle of her eyebrows.

"How do you think I ended up with Eloise?" Henrietta giggled, her usually serene and stately face pinking. "Your brother has what I believe is called an Irish temper. And I wouldn't have it any other way."

"Fighting is half the fun of being married," Colleen said with a coy shrug of one shoulder.

Shannon still wasn't sure. She hadn't enjoyed anything about her fight with Colin. Particularly since she was convinced she hadn't come out of it smelling like roses. Although Colin was no saint either, she rushed to defend herself. They had both lost their tempers and—

Her thought was cut short as she spotted Mr. Doherty stepping into the church at the far end of the hall within her line of sight with a woman who must have been his wife. Shannon's eyes popped wider when Colin stepped in behind them. They were too far away for her to hear what they were saying, but Colin seemed to be gesturing to Mr. Doherty as though selling him something, perhaps selling him an idea.

Shannon stood abruptly, anger washing over her again. She'd let Colin help with her brewing efforts. She'd shared her recipes with him. Colin had worked at a vineyard, so he knew something of the sort of business she was involved in. The whelp couldn't be attempting to go behind her back with Mr. Doherty, could he?

No, Colin would never do that to her.

But why else would he be speaking with Doherty?

Shannon hurried forward, marching out of the room and ignoring her sisters' strange looks and questions. She headed straight down the hall, her head of steam already building, even before she reached the men.

Mr. Doherty spotted her first, glancing past Colin's shoulder to say, "Ah, Lady Shannon. Mr. Crenshaw and I were just speaking about you." He bent to whisper something to his wife, who nodded sagely and left them to continue on into the church.

"I'd wager you were," Shannon said through a clenched jaw, nodding briefly to Mrs. Doherty.

Colin nearly jumped when he realized she was right behind him. "Shannon," he said, his face passing through a whirlwind of expressions, his eyes lighting with love and hope, then caution and wariness. "We were, in fact, discussing you."

"And what, pray tell, were you saying?" she asked, crossing her arms.

Mr. Doherty cleared his throat. "I understand that Mr. Crenshaw is not your business partner, as I was previously led to believe," he said, looking grave.

"Whether I have any connection to this man or not is irrelevant," Shannon snapped. "Were you able to read the proposal I gave you, Mr. Doherty, and did you find it to your liking?"

"I did read it, Lady Shannon," Mr. Doherty said. "I was impressed with it as well. You have a strong idea and the means to make it grow."

"But?" she asked, seeing the hesitation in his eyes.

"But I cannot go into business with a single lady of your stature," Mr. Doherty said. "Particularly this sort of business."

Shannon wanted to scream and cry. She glared at Colin. He had probably gone to Mr. Doherty to explain everything and ruin it all in the process, as he was want to do.

"As I have been telling Mr. Doherty since I encountered him on the way to the wedding," Colin contradicted her thoughts in clipped tones, staring hard at Shannon as if to force her to realize he was advocating for her, "business is business, regardless of who conducts it. Your plan is a solid one, and he would be a fool to pass it up simply because the brilliant mind who conceived of it is a female one." He finished by staring hard at Mr. Doherty.

"Be that as it may," Mr. Doherty said with a sigh, holding up his hands, "the complications of doing business with a single woman of any sort are too much for me to risk my own business. If the two of you were partners in business—or partners in other things—we would have more to talk about."

"It is not fair that Shannon be held down simply because of her sex or birth," Colin defended her, taking the words out of Shannon's mouth even as she opened her mouth to speak. She blinked at him in surprise. "Even you must admit that the beer Shannon brews is second to none."

The glowing compliment came just as Lord and Lady Wallingsford entered the church, Fergus wheeling his way in right behind them.

"Your beer is excellent," Mr. Doherty admitted. Lord Wallingsford looked aghast at the statement. "Better than most. And your business acumen also appears to be sharper than many of the men I've dealt with." Lord Wallingsford looked even more alarmed, as though Mr. Doherty's statements might be in danger of causing him to have a brain seizure. "But I must remain firm. In spite of your persistent efforts, I cannot do business with a woman."

"Business?" Lord Wallingsford boomed. "What is this nonsense?"

Colin pressed his fingertips to the bridge of his nose and clenched his jaw for a moment before answering, "As I tried to explain the other night, Shannon is an accomplished brewer and business-woman, Father. She has been working hard these last few weeks to expand her business and to find a partner to help her do so."

Lord Wallingsford's face had gone red, and his moustache quivered. "You are in business with this woman?" he demanded of Mr. Doherty.

Mr. Doherty looked as though he were about to be raked across hot coals. "In fact, my lord, I am not. And I am suddenly of a mind not to attend this wedding, no matter how grand of a social occasion it is. If you will excuse me. Tell my wife I had business elsewhere." He bowed, then hurried out of the church so quickly any passerby would have thought there was a fire.

"That was uncalled for, Father," Colin snapped.

"No, Stamford, what is uncalled for is you engaging yourself to an aberration of a woman, such as this," Lord Wallingsford said.

"That is my sister," Fergus attempted to defend her.

"And you should keep a closer eye on her, sir," Lord Wallingsford clipped. He scowled at Fergus. "Were you the one who allowed the chit to engage in business?"

"She did it without my permission, my lord," Fergus growled, "but I am beginning to see that I am, in fact, excessively proud of her."

It was the right praise coming at the wrong time. "If you are so proud of me, why did you not help me instead of hindering me?" Shannon demanded.

Fergus opened his mouth, but Lord Wallingsford cut him off with, "I have changed my mind." He glanced to his wife, then to Colin. "This marriage cannot happen.

Regardless of the consequences, I cannot allow you to continue to engage yourself to a harridan involved in *business*"—he spoke the word as though Shannon were involved in murder—"who has nothing better than some insignificant, Irish earldom to recommend her."

Fergus's one eye flashed wide. "And I demand you call the wedding off as well, because I will not have myself or my family connected to any preening, self-important, shites of English marquessates."

"How dare you?" Lady Wallingsford clapped a hand to her chest.

"This marriage is over," Fergus said, glaring from Lord Wallingsford to Colin to Shannon, then wheeling himself angrily into the sanctuary.

"It most certainly is over," Lord Wallingsford agreed. He narrowed his eyes at Colin and said, "I expect you to return to your duties as the Wallingsford heir as soon as we return to England. You will socialize with the right people, you will take up membership in the right club, and you will find yourself a suitable Englishwoman to marry. If you do not before this time next year, I will search out one for you."

He nodded to punctuate his statement, then stuck out his elbow to Lady Wallingsford. She took it, tilted up her chin with a high-pitched, "Hmph," and the two of them headed into the sanctuary as well.

Shannon was left staring after them all, her mind reeling, no idea if she wanted to shout in victory over the fact that the engagement that she'd never consented to in the first place was over, or whether she wanted to weep because Colin was out of her reach forever. The conflicting emotions left her numb and unable to do anything but blink and feel small.

Colin, however, appeared to have other ideas.

"Come on," he said, grabbing her hand and attempting to pull her toward the door and out into the street. "We don't have much time."

Shannon wrenched her hand out of his grip. "What in blazes do you think you're doing, you madman?"

Colin's expression flared with excitement, but also impatience. He reached for her hand again. "Come on," he repeated, managing to pull her outside in earnest. "We have to catch up to Doherty before he dips out of sight and we've lost him for good."

"Mr. Doherty?" Shannon balked, but let herself be dragged on.

"Yes," Colin said, nearly shouting. "We have to catch up to him. And once we do, we're going to save your brewery."

CHAPTER 11

*A*s far as humiliations at the hands of his father went, the scene at the church was not particularly bad. His father had insulted Shannon, humiliated him yet again, and attempted to order his life as though he were a child while O'Shea and whoever else happened to be entering the church for the wedding at the time looked on, but his words had also been the last straw. And there was nothing quite so freeing as the last straw being plucked and tossed to the floor.

"Where are we going?" Shannon demanded, looking as though she couldn't decide whether to be furious, hurt, or just stunned as Colin dragged her out to the street, then looked this way and that. "Colin, unhand me at once. This is madness. My sister is about to be married, and I am her maid of honor."

Colin spotted what he was looking for—or rather whom he was looking for—on the other side of the street, nearly a block down. Doherty hadn't walked far away from the church after their conversation, but he'd moved quickly enough. He was still in sight for the moment, but there was no telling how long that moment would last.

"Hurry," he told Shannon, tugging her along into the street and dodging a passing carriage that he hadn't fully seen in the process.

Shannon yelped at the carriage, but kept up with him as they dashed to the opposite street. "Stop right now, Colin," she shouted at him. "I'm not dressed for running about the streets. I don't have a coat or a hat and—oh!" She yelped again as Colin dragged her past a vendor selling roasted nuts, forcing her to dodge the man. "What are we doing?"

Colin could tell by the way she attempted to pull her hand out of his and dig in her heels that she wanted to stop for explanations, but there simply wasn't time. "Look ahead. There's Doherty. If we don't hurry, he'll get away."

Shannon made a growling sound, as if trying to decide whether to commit to joining Colin's chase, then hurried along with him. "I fail to see the point. Mr. Doherty has made his position clear. He will not do business with a woman. He has made up his mind."

"Then we will convince him to unmake it," Colin called over his shoulder to her.

His spirits rose with exhilaration the more they ran, ducking and diving around pedestrians passing the other way and vendors and hawkers set up near the street corners. Doherty seemed oblivious to the fact that he was being chased, even though everyone Colin and Shannon passed gaped and gasped at them as they leapt out of the way.

When they finally caught up with Doherty just as he was about to enter a pub three streets away from the church, Colin called out, "Doherty! Doherty, wait!"

Doherty paused in confusion, glanced around, and when he spotted Colin and Shannon racing toward him, his brow flew up. "Mr. Crenshaw? Lady Shannon? What is the meaning of this?"

Colin burst into a grin. He found it amusing that Doherty had caught on to Shannon being a lady, but he still thought Colin was simply a mister. There would be time to laugh over that later, though.

"I would like to know the meaning of this as well," Shannon demanded, out of breath, pink-cheeked from running, and looking as beautiful as Colin had ever seen her—excepting when he'd seen her naked.

Doherty glanced to Shannon as though the two of them were on the same side, for a change, and they both looked to Colin.

"Mr. Doherty," Colin began in a more businesslike voice—marred only by his panting as he caught his breath, "I cannot allow you to walk away from what may very well be the most lucrative and exciting business opportunity that will ever come your way."

Shannon widened her eyes at Colin, as if she couldn't believe what he was doing.

Doherty looked more anxious about the scene they were causing than what Colin had actually said. "Perhaps we should go inside and discuss the matter there," he said.

"Agreed," Colin said. He leapt ahead to hold the pub's door for Shannon, then gestured for Doherty to precede him inside.

There was a moment of fuss as Doherty glanced around, looking for a table that might accommodate them, but before he could take in much of the room, Colin stepped around, grabbed Shannon's hand, and addressed him right in the pub's entryway.

"Mr. Doherty, you have read Lady Shannon's business proposal. I assume you have tasted her beer. You have seen for yourself that she is the most indomitable woman you will ever meet," Colin began. "You cannot imagine that those traits do not translate into a head for business and brewing that will take your business as it stands now and lift it to higher realms of success."

"Colin, what are you doing?" Shannon hissed. She turned to Doherty. "I am so sorry, Mr. Doherty. I did not ask Mr. Crenshaw to do this. He is acting of his own accord."

Colin's heart leapt in his chest at the use of his surname, not his title. She was giving him the benefit of the doubt, not exposing him straight away as an earl, which could dissuade Doherty from everything he was saying.

"No," he said, shaking his head. "Lady Shannon did

not ask me to speak on her behalf," he told Doherty. "I speak of my own free will, because I believe in what she is doing with my whole heart, and with every bit of business acumen I possess. I worked for a summer at a vineyard in France, learning not only about the production of wine, but the business of it as well, and I can tell you that Lady Shannon's understanding of this sort of industry is well beyond what you will find even in the most seasoned professional."

"I...I could tell that from the proposal," Doherty said, his expression unreadable.

Shannon still seemed upset, as if she didn't know what to make of Colin's dogged determination on her behalf or the fact that Doherty hadn't dismissed her outright yet.

Colin turned to her fully, taking her hands, his heart thumping in his throat. "I have made more than my fair share of mistakes in my young life," he said, gazing at her with all the mad passion he felt for her clearly on display. "I have done things I shouldn't have and not done things I should've. And the worst of it is, I'm still young and have years of making moronic mistakes ahead of me."

"Colin." Shannon's eyes softened, but tension continued to ripple off of her. She peeked anxiously to Doherty, who watched the scene with interest and the barest hint of amusement in his eyes.

"I am more of a burden than a blessing when all is said and done," Colin went on, "but I know greatness when I see it. I believe in you and what you are doing. I cannot allow you to give up on this business that you have built—built beautifully and expertly, even though women are purported not to be able to do such things, which is pure poppycock, if you ask me." He glanced briefly to Doherty. "What does it matter if she is a woman when she is so magnificent at everything she does?"

"You may have a point," Doherty said, though it was still unclear what he really thought from his tone.

Colin glanced back to Shannon, unable to keep his smile in check. "Shannon, you are loveliness personified, and you are strength incarnate. I cannot decide if I have cocked everything up for you or if I have helped, but you must know that all I want to do is help. I believe in you, because you are the only person who has ever made me feel as though you believe in me."

He faced Doherty again. "Throwing your lot in with Shannon would be the single most brilliant decision you could ever make, Mr. Doherty. I chased after you just now, dragging Shannon away from her own sister's wedding, because I believe that with my whole heart. The two of you would make perfect partners—but business partners only, because if I have my way, the other sort of partnership that a woman may become involved in is already mine and mine alone."

"Colin, you irascible fool," Shannon sighed, blinking rapidly.

The moment was beautiful beyond measure, and Colin was sorely tempted to pull Shannon to him and kiss her to prove how deeply he loved her, but the entire scene was interrupted as a barrel-chested man wearing an apron marched forward from the back of the pub.

"What in blazes is going on—" he began, then stopped short, his expression softening into a smile at the sight of Shannon. "Forgive me, Lady Shannon, I didn't recognize it was you at first, dressed as beautifully as you are."

"Good morning, Mr. Coney," Shannon greeted the man, her face red with embarrassment, looking apologetically at the man. "I am terribly sorry to disturb your establishment like this."

Both Colin and Doherty glanced in confusion from Shannon to Mr. Coney.

"You know this woman?" Doherty asked Mr. Coney.

"Know her? Of course I do," Mr. Coney said with a broad smile. "Lady Shannon is my best supplier. My patrons are always asking if her beer is in stock."

"Mr. Coney is the owner of The Hangman Pub," Shannon said, gesturing around to show that was where they were.

Colin and Doherty stared at her in unison, both surprised, but perhaps for different reasons.

"I never expected to see you darkening my doorstep on your sister's wedding day," Mr. Coney went on. "And certainly not in the pub itself. We usually do our dealings in my office," he noted for Mr. Doherty. "Lady Shannon is the shrewdest brewer I deal with. She won't budge in her pricing for anything, but her wares are in such high demand that I'll pay whatever she asks." He blinked, then glanced to Shannon with a grin. "I probably shouldn't have told you that. Now you'll bilk me at every chance you get." He winked at her for good measure.

Shannon let out a breath and her shoulders dropped in what Colin could only describe as relief. "I would never deal falsely with you, Mr. Coney," she said with a smile.

"I know, my lady," Mr. Coney smiled at her. "I was only teasing." He nudged Doherty's arm, as though he were in on the joke as well. "When do you think you'll have your next shipment ready, my lady?" he went on. "Customers keep asking for it. Jerry Parsons wants to buy a whole case of bottles for consumption at home as well."

"I—" Shannon glanced uncertainly at Doherty, then at Colin. "I'm not entirely certain, Mr. Coney. Production has slowed down a bit due to...to my sister's wedding."

"Understandable." Mr. Coney nodded.

"Am I to understand that you have been doing business with Lady Shannon?" Doherty asked Mr. Coney, curiosity flashing in his eyes.

"Indeed, I have," Mr. Coney said.

"In spite of the fact that she's a woman?" Doherty asked on.

Mr. Coney made a scoffing sound. "What do I care? Her beer is excellent and she's a fair and honest business-woman." He shrugged.

"And you would vouch for her, as a client, I mean?" Doherty asked on.

"I would give her my uninhibited endorsement, yes, sir," Mr. Coney said with a nod. His expression changed to curiosity, and he asked, "Why? Who are you?"

Doherty glanced from Mr. Coney to Shannon, a smile forming across his face. "I am her new business partner, sir," he said. "Lady Shannon and I are about to embark on an effort to merge our businesses so that her beer can be produced on a larger scale and distributed to more pubs."

Shannon made a sound as though she might burst into tears and raised a hand to her mouth. Colin felt as though his heart might leap straight out of his chest and soar up to the heavens.

Mr. Coney, however, looked concerned. "This won't affect the quality of the product will it?" he asked, glancing between Doherty and Shannon. "I trust Lady Shannon," he went on. "I do not know you yet, sir. I might prefer to continue doing business with the lady, since she has never done me wrong before."

Doherty's smile grew. "I can assure you, Mr. Coney, that I will consider Lady Shannon as a full and equal partner. I can see that she has done a capital job of cultivating her clients and forming bonds of trust with them. That is a skill that cannot easily be duplicated."

"Then I look forward to doing business with you both," Mr. Coney said. "And if you will excuse me, I have a great deal of work to get done before lunchtime."

"Of course, Mr. Coney," Shannon said. "And thank you so much." She had to blink back tears as she spoke.

Colin fully understood why. He might have dragged the horse to water, but Mr. Coney was the one who had made it drink.

"Forgive me for failing to trust in you sooner, Lady Shannon," Doherty said with a bow. "But now, I believe you have a wedding to attend. I will contact you after Christmas to set up a meeting so that we might discuss the merger further."

"Thank you, Mr. Doherty," Shannon said, a bit breathlessly. She took Doherty's hand when he offered it to shake. "I look forward to our partnership."

"Do you know, Lady Shannon," Doherty said with a smile, "I believe I do as well. Especially considering that you have another partner who, I have seen, will gladly go to the ends of the earth to support you in your endeavors." He nodded to Colin. "Now, if you will excuse me, I think perhaps I will attend your sister's wedding after all. It is the social event of the season, as I have been given to understand."

They said their goodbyes, and Doherty left. Shannon turned to go after him, but Colin grabbed her hand and held her to her place. For a moment, Shannon seemed unwilling to look up at him.

"I am so glad that Mr. Doherty changed his mind about going into business with me," she said, almost bashfully, "but I am sorry that he misunderstood the nature of our...partnership."

"I don't think he misunderstood anything," Colin

said, tugging her around to face him fully, mischief coursing through him.

Shannon let out an impatient breath and glanced up, meeting his eyes. "Colin," she said in that scolding tone that drove him wild with love and lust.

"Shannon," he gave the scolding right back to her.

She broke into a reluctant smile. "You are an impossible whelp," she said, but there was a great deal of affection in her tone.

Colin grabbed hold of that affection, and both of her hands. "I meant it when I said that I have done a great many things wrong," he said, gazing into her eyes with all the joy and guilt in his heart. "But I confess it is because I'm too young to know what I'm doing in love." He paused, then said, "That is to say, I know what I am doing in some regards." He flickered one eyebrow lasciviously.

Shannon laughed out loud, then clapped a hand to her mouth. "Yes, you do know what you're doing in some regards."

"But in others, I need someone older and wiser to guide and shape me," he said, pulling her closer and gazing into her eyes with all of the love he felt coursing through him. "I need someone who can give my life purpose by giving me something real to work toward, not just a silly title and the idle expectations that go along with it. I need someone who understands and who will not judge me for wanting to get my hands dirty. I need you."

She blinked rapidly, holding back tears, at his declaration. "I may be loathe to admit it," she said, "but I believe I have been convinced that I need you as well, you impossible fool."

"Good," he said. He couldn't help but pull her into his embrace, slanting his mouth over hers and kissing her with all the affection that had his heart—and more —throbbing.

Their kiss stopped when one of the pub's patrons called out in victory, proving that their entire scene was being witnessed. Part of Colin loved it, though.

"Did you like that?" he asked the older man sitting at a table a few yards away from them.

"Aye, I did," the man said, holding up his pint.

"Then you'll love this." Colin dropped to one knee, still holding Shannon's hands. She gasped, but he charged on with, "Shannon O'Shea, I have loved you from the moment I laid eyes on you. And if you will recall, I have already made this proposal once. But I also failed to make it when I truly should have. I pray that you will forgive me, and with your whole heart that you will agree when I ask you now to marry me, be my wife, my life, my heart, and my soul."

"Oh, Colin," she said, seeming to melt with affection in front of him. A moment later, she gasped and her back snapped straight. She squeezed his hands hard and said, "Oh! Colin! The wedding!"

Colin leapt to his feet, energized by her alarm. "What about it?"

Her eyes went wide, and she tugged him to the door.

"The wedding. It's happening now. They need us there. We are supposed to be at the church."

"Then we'll fly off to the church and I'll get my answer later," Colin said, dashing ahead of her to hold open the door.

CHAPTER 12

Shannon's entire body buzzed with about a dozen different kinds of excitement as she and Colin raced back through the streets of Ballymena to the church. Mr. Doherty was willing to do business with her after all. Mr. Coney had been amazingly kind when he stood up for her. And Colin had taken her breath away when he knelt down for her. The whole thing spun her head to the point where she nearly tripped over herself as Colin helped her across the busy street, then took her hand as they dashed toward the church. The whole thing was such a whirlwind that she couldn't think.

Unsurprisingly, the church was chaotic when she and Colin stumbled back through the front door.

"Good God, man! Where have you been?" Blackburn gasped in relief—and irritation—as he spotted Colin. "And you too, Lady Shannon. Chloe is frantic without you."

"I'm sorry," Shannon panted, letting go of Colin's hand and veering off toward the room where her sisters were waiting. "You will explain to him, won't you?" she asked Colin as Blackburn grabbed his arm and practically goose-stepped him into the sanctuary. The only answer Shannon got was a silly, lovesick look from Colin as he blew her a kiss and was dragged away.

Shannon resisted the urge to laugh as she scrambled down the hall to the room where her sisters were waiting.

"There you are," Chloe gasped, flying to her from the corner of the room, where she'd been pacing. "I didn't know what happened to you," she went on, almost as breathless as Shannon was. "One moment you were there and the next you weren't, and the wedding was supposed to begin fifteen minutes ago, and why are you all dewy and out of breath?" Her thoughts flew faster than Shannon could keep up with them, and her green eyes were huge with worry.

"Never you mind now, dearest," Shannon told her, sending apologetic looks to Marie and Colleen as well. "I will explain all later. The very best of things have happened while I was gone. But for now, it is time for you to marry your duke."

Chloe's anxious look vanished, and she made an excited sound, positively glowing. Henrietta had returned to the doorway from whatever errand she'd been away on and gestured for Chloe to come out to the hall, that it was time for the ceremony to begin. They followed her out to the doorway near the back of the sanctuary,

Marie and Colleen slipped in to take their places with their husbands, and when the music wafting out from the sanctuary changed, Shannon quickly moved to kiss Chloe's cheek.

"I'm so sorry to have nearly spoiled your special day," she whispered. "I love you dearly, and I am so proud of the woman you have become."

"Oh," Chloe squealed. "Do not make me cry. I am already inches away from turning into a watering can as it is."

Shannon laughed, kissed her cheek again, then turned to proceed down the aisle.

She couldn't believe how much her life had changed in less than a fortnight. She had been so certain that she'd known precisely what path she was on and what the scenery along that road would be. She was convinced that the independent life of a businesswoman was the life for her. Now she knew two things in her heart—that she would never have been able to succeed with her brewery on her own, unfair though that was, but also that she loved Lord Colin Crenshaw, Earl of Stamford, with her whole heart, and that she wanted to spend the rest of her life as his countess.

He looked so handsome, standing up at the front of the church alongside Blackburn as he did. Even though his hair was a mess, his face was still red from running, and his suit was slightly rumpled. She liked him that way, liked him unfettered and unfinished. The idea of picking him up, brushing him off, and putting him to work excited her in ways that she didn't entirely understand. All she knew as she approached the front of the church and stepped to the side, ready to perform her maid of honor duties, was that nothing in the world would stop her from marrying Colin.

"Dearly beloved, we are gathered here today to celebrate the marriage of Lord Deane Crenshaw, Duke of Blackburn, to Lady Chloe O'Shea," the celebrant began.

The words were familiar to Shannon from every wedding she'd ever attended, but they reverberated through her with deeper meaning as she glanced across to Colin. His impish smile and the cheeky flash in his eyes made it next to impossible for her to pay attention to the service, as beautiful as she always found weddings to be.

"Will you, Deane Crenshaw, take this woman, Chloe O'Shea, to be your lawfully wedded wife," the celebrant continued.

Shannon gazed across at Colin, his proposal welling up within her. He'd spoken with such feeling and such certainty. He always spoke with feeling and certainty, and without fear or intimidation. He might have been young, but he had the confidence of a man of experience, a confidence she liked.

"...I now pronounce you man and wife."

Shannon blinked as Chloe and Blackburn kissed each other. She'd been so caught up in her love for Colin that she'd missed everything. Knowing that made her determined never to miss anything again.

The celebrant opened his mouth to move on with the ceremony, but Shannon held up a hand and said, "Wait!"

The celebrant looked as though he might choke on whatever it was he had planned to say next. Chloe and Blackburn turned to her, and it felt as though everyone in the church was gaping at her.

"Wait," she repeated in a marginally softer voice, glancing across to Colin. "I would like you to marry me to Lord Stamford as well."

A slight gasp and a round of murmurs followed as the congregation turned to each other in shock.

The celebrant's mouth flapped for a moment before he said, "My lady, the banns have not been read, nor a special license produced."

"What if a special license was produced?" Colin asked, stepping forward, his eyes shining as he smiled at Shannon.

The celebrant—and Chloe and Blackburn—blinked in surprise. "Do you have one?" he asked.

Colin's smile widened. "Er, no, I do not. I was just wondering."

"You daft fool." Shannon stepped forward to grasp his hand. She turned to the celebrant. "Could you perform the ceremony without it? So we could be married in the eyes of God, if not legally yet?"

"It is highly, highly unusual," the celebrant said, shuffling in his spot, wincing, then looking to Blackburn, as if a duke held the answers to ecclesiastical and legal matters.

163

Blackburn rolled his eyes at his cousin, grinning, and sighed to the celebrant, "Why not? I know it isn't legal and that we'll have to take care of the details later, but could you, perhaps, let them speak vows to one another?"

"I...I...I suppose so?" The celebrant let out a breath and smiled at Shannon and Colin. "I always did adore a good love story."

More murmurs followed from the congregation as Chloe and Blackburn stepped to one side, letting Shannon and Colin take their places.

"Dearly beloved," the celebrant began again. "We are—"

"What in God's name are you doing?" Lord Wallingsford bellowed, standing from his front-row pew. He glared at Colin.

It was the celebrant who answered, "I am joining these two impetuous young people in marriage. That is what I am doing in God's name."

"I absolutely forbid it," Lord Wallingsford boomed.

Shannon glanced to Fergus, to see what he thought of the whole thing. Her brother merely sat back in his wheelchair at the end of the pew opposite Lord Wallingsford, arms crossed, grinning as though he were curious to see how the final act of the comedy unfurled.

"I do not care if you forbid it," Colin said, turning to his father and standing tall. "I do not care what you think of the choices I have made in my life. It is my life to choose."

"Impudent fool," Lord Wallingsford growled. "If you

do this thing, I will never speak to you again. Your name will be struck from the family Bible. I will no longer be your father. You will never be welcomed at Wallingsford Park again."

"Thank God," Colin exclaimed, glancing up to the ceiling, as though he'd received a boon directly from heaven. "I have never felt at home there anyhow. You have never seen me as your son, or as a man with thoughts and feelings of his own, so it isn't as though you have been my father to begin with. In these few short days, Shannon has shown me more love and encouragement than you ever have." He glanced to Shannon with a smile. "I would be a fool not to marry her and embrace everything she means to me every day for the rest of my life."

Shannon was certain she heard a few of the ladies in the congregation sigh.

"If you choose to do this, then on your head be it," Lord Wallingsford grumbled. He reached for his wife's hand and yanked her to her feet. "You will never see either of us again."

Colin held his ground, back straight, expression firm. "Goodbye," he said, simple and without either victory or venom.

Lord Wallingsford gave him one last look, as though he couldn't believe Colin would be so stubborn, then slipped his wife's hand into the crook of his arm and marched out of the church with her.

"Don't worry," Colin said as he rested his hand on the

small of Shannon's back and turned her to face the celebrant again. "He cannot disown me entirely. British inheritance law won't allow it. We'll be forced to see them again whenever a formal occasion presents itself."

"Perish the thought," Shannon muttered.

The two of them exchanged a look, then burst into laughter.

The service that the celebrant threw together from there had every hallmark of being a slap-dash, improvised effort, but Shannon didn't care. Even though the vows were rushed and the celebrant stumbled over his words as he tried to join them together without overstepping his bounds and saying something that might imply the ceremony had any legal standing at all, it was beautiful. Shannon got to express her love for Colin in front of half the population of Ballymena, and Colin got to do the same.

"I was certain the police would smash through the doors at the back of the church and drag the two of you off," Cousin Angeline laughed to them hours later, after the wedding luncheon Marie and Christian had hosted at Kilrea Manor.

"I don't think I've ever seen anything like it," Cousin Caelian said as their family group stood around, laughing about what had everyone on tenterhooks at the church. "And here I thought I was the eccentric in our family, what with my flying machine and all."

"Believe me, this family has more eccentrics than

most," Cousin Avery said, glancing across to his sister, Angeline, and her new husband, Lord Rothbury.

"As I have come to learn," Lord Rothbury said.

"But you must admit, dearest," Lady Angeline said, holding his arm and gazing adoringly up at him, "we do keep things interesting."

"We do indeed," Lord Rothbury grinned adoringly back at her.

"And Lord Stamford here appears to fit right in with the rest of us," Cousin Caelian said, nodding to Colin with a grin.

"I most certainly do," Colin said. He raised his and Shannon's joined hands to his lips, kissing her knuckles lovingly.

"I suppose you have plans to make this surprise marriage of yours fully legal as soon as possible?" Cousin Avery asked.

"We most certainly do," Colin said, glancing mischievously at Shannon. "In fact, I have a few ideas of how we can speed the process of making this the most real of real marriages as quickly as possible."

"Oh?" Shannon asked, reasonably convinced he was teasing, but curious to see what he had in mind. "Do you?"

"I do," Colin said, then stood straighter, his expression lighting with surprise and delight. "See? I have begun already."

The family group laughed.

"Tell me more," Shannon said in her best voice of command.

She saw the amorous effect of her words in Colin's flashing eyes. "I will," he said, "but not here. Come with me."

"Excuse me," Shannon said to her cousins, letting Colin lead her away from the conversation.

She was somewhat startled when he led her out of the ballroom where the reception was being held and along to the grand staircase at the front of the house. As soon as he started up those stairs, though, her heart leapt in excitement as she guessed what Colin had in mind.

"Colin, we cannot," she whispered, face heating as she hurried up the stairs with him. "It is the middle of the day, the middle of Chloe and Blackburn's reception."

"It is the perfect time to slip away and make our marriage official," Colin insisted as he pulled her along the hall to the guestroom he was currently occupying.

"Consummating the marriage will not make it legally official," she insisted, even as he opened his bedchamber door and tugged her inside.

"No," he said as he shut the door, then turned to wedge her against it, "but it certainly will be fun."

He brought his mouth crashing over hers in a kiss that was so filled with passion and enthusiasm Shannon couldn't resist it. She kissed him back through her laughter, looping her arms over his shoulders and leaning into him. Colin was as wild and puckish as they came, but she wouldn't have traded him for any other man in the world.

"I could stand here and kiss you all day," he hummed against her lips, brushing his tongue along her bottom lip, then sucking her tongue into his mouth for a moment. His hands roved her body, searching out the fastenings of her bridesmaid's gown as he did. "I *could*," he went on, "but I would so much rather lie there and make love to you all day." He inched back from her and winked.

"Who am I to argue with a well-thought-out plan such as that?" Shannon teased him, going immediately to work on the buttons of his suit jacket.

They made their way slowly across the room to the bed, undressing bit by bit as they did. Clothes were the most annoying hindrance to love that Shannon could think of, but they both managed to divest each other of their finery piece by piece until the floor of Colin's guestroom looked like a particularly sloppy laundry. Shannon didn't think a thing of it as Colin pulled back the covers on his bed, hooked her around the waist, and dragged her between the cool sheets until she was on her back, gazing up at him, her legs open around his hips.

"This is quite an interesting position for a business-woman of such renown to find herself in," Colin hummed as he brushed his fingers up her side, sending shivers and gasps through Shannon, then closed his hand around one of her breasts to knead it. "Not at all how you would expect to find a triumphant brewery owner." He leaned down to kiss her with a passion that took Shannon's breath away.

"I don't know about that," Shannon purred, arching

into his touch, especially as he trailed kisses down her neck and over her shoulder to meet his hand on her breast. "I think it is entirely fitting to celebrate a day of successes in as intimate a manner as possible."

Colin laughed as he closed his mouth over her nipple, which sent a jolt of fascinating sensation through her that vibrated in her core. In an instant, she was aching for him. She wriggled against him, asking for more.

Colin glanced up, slightly breathless, and gazed at her with fire in her eyes. "My, my, Mrs. Crenshaw, you certainly are wanton this afternoon, aren't you?"

Shannon hummed in delight, lifting her arms over her head. "I love everything about what you just said," she sighed. "Particularly the 'Mrs. Crenshaw' part."

"Do you?" More mischief sparkled in his eyes. "Then I wonder how you will like this."

He kissed his way down from her breast, across her belly, and along one of her thighs. Shannon was already giddy with pleasure, but the touch of his lips and the brush of his tongue only made her want it more. She panted and wriggled breathlessly as he pushed her thighs farther apart, and trailed his fingers up her overly-sensitive flesh to her sex. Part of her expected him to tease her for a moment, but he seemed as eager for pleasure as she was and stroked her open, exploring her with his fingers.

"Oh, Colin," she panted, arching into him. "That feels so good."

"I don't know how long I can keep it up, though," he

said, his voice rich with passion. "You're so erotically beautiful that I can hardly help myself."

"Then don't," Shannon said, phrasing it like an order. "I demand that you bring me to climax and then take your own right now."

"Your wish is my command, my darling," he replied, a hint of laughter in his voice.

Shannon would have laughed in return, but that laughter turned to a moan of pleasure as he brought his mouth to her and flickered his tongue over the parts of her that wanted him most. He was devilishly skilled in that regard, and she was no match for the onslaught of pleasure that overtook her. She wriggled and gasped, stretching her legs open wider so that he could have every last bit of her, then let out a cry of pleasure as her body burst into starlight and wonder as it gave in to him.

"My darling," Colin growled, slipping his body back up over hers and bringing his mouth to hers.

He didn't hesitate at all, pushing inside of her before her orgasm was even finished. For a beautiful moment, they hung there together, her body squeezing its last around Colin as his mouth ravished hers. It was perfect and intimate and beautiful, and then the moment shone even brighter as he began to move.

"I adore you, Shannon," Colin gasped as his thrusts grew faster and harder. "You are the world to me."

"And you are to me," she echoed, crying out in time to his thrusts as her body held on to the scintillating pleasure he gave her. "I love you so much."

His response was little more than an impassioned groan as he thrust, panting and vocalizing that love as he did. She didn't even mind that he couldn't last more than a minute or so, spilling himself into her with a cry of delight. It was perfect, wonderful, and beautiful, and they would have more than enough time to pleasure each other silly for hours, days, and years to come.

"I cannot imagine anything better than this," Shannon sighed happily as he collapsed into her arms. She hugged and kissed him as he settled against her, as if he'd found his home. "You are my darling, Colin, and I will never let you forget it.

The cottage had never looked so beautiful. Even though the front garden, around the door, was littered with bits and pieces of brewing equipment, as well as Colin's trunks and traveling bags.

"That should be the last of it," Cousin Caelian said as he helped Colin move the last trunk. "Are you certain there isn't anything else you want brought down from the castle, Shannon?" he asked on, brushing off his hands and moving to where Shannon stood in the doorway.

"If we need anything else, I'm sure Fergus will lend us a footman to bring it down," Shannon said with a contented smile.

"We have to sort out what we have first." Colin moved to stand beside her, sliding an arm around her waist and hugging her close in the icy, January breeze. "And then we have to decide what two businesspeople need to stock their cozy little home."

Shannon grinned at him, her heart brimming with adoration, then glanced up at the cottage. It had been a matter of course that she and Colin would make their home in the cottage. Colin had an entire estate in England, but seeing as neither of them had any intention of setting foot over there for more than a fleeting holiday and to make certain the estate didn't crash to the ground, they'd needed a home. And while most of her brewing operation was in the process of being transferred to a larger facility in Ballymena, now that the ink was dry on her contract with Mr. Doherty, space within the cottage had freed up to make it a true home once more.

"I'm surprised Fergus didn't force you to stay in Dunegard Castle, once all of the legalities of your marriage were worked out," Caelian went on with a bright smile. "That's all of his sisters gone from him within a year."

"Oh, believe me, he is positively crowing over getting rid of all of us," Shannon laughed. "At last, he and Henrietta and their little family can spend some time together."

"I hear Fergus's friends, Lord and Lady Marlowe and Lord Howsden and his friend, Lord Herrington will be coming over for a time this spring," Colin said.

"And bringing young Lord Henry so that he and my sister-in-law's son, Ricky, can be reunited. The two are close friends," Shannon went on. "So don't you worry about Fergus getting lonely. In fact, I'd dare say—"

Shannon's words were cut off as a brightly-colored paper kite came sailing into the yard and nearly crashed straight into Caelian. In fact, Caelian had to duck and cover his head to keep from having an eye poked out.

A moment later, a high-pitched squeak of, "Oh! Oh, I'm so sorry. Please forgive me," followed the attacking kite.

Shannon glanced to the side to find a young woman with dark brown hair, her cheeks pink from the cold and exertion, wearing a simple, grey woolen coat over an even simpler brown skirt, come tearing up from the beach. She held one hand clamped to a straw hat on her head, and in the other she held a large spool of string.

In an instant, Shannon assessed that the woman was the owner of the kite, that she was English, judging by her accent on the few words she's spoken, and that Cousin Caelian had been hit by more than just the kite. He looked positively dumbstruck.

"You seem to have lost something," Colin said, stepping away from Shannon with an impish look that said he, too, had noticed Caelian's reaction. He moved to retrieve the woman's kite from one of the dormant rose bushes, where it had ended up.

Caelian continued to stand where he was, gaping at the woman.

"I am ever so sorry," the Englishwoman said, focused mostly on Shannon, but glancing to Colin in thanks as he returned her kite. She also peeked at Caelian, and her already pink cheeks went even pinker. "I do so love to fly kites, and the beach seemed like the perfect place for it. I am still uncertain about where I can or should fly in the area, as my father and I have just moved to town. He is the new parson at St. Cuthbert's, Mr. Joyce. We only just arrived shortly before Christmas and are hardly settled, but the wind seemed so favorable today, and I simply had to get out and—" She stopped abruptly, putting her free hand to her mouth. "Oh, dear. I've talked your ear off already, and we've only just met. I am sorry. I have a tendency to prattle on. My name is Erica Joyce, by the way."

"It's quite all right," Shannon said with a smile, extending her hand. "Lady Shannon—" Shannon stopped, turning to Colin, her eyes wide. "I do believe this is the first time I've introduced myself by my married name," she said, beaming. She turned back to Miss Joyce with, "Lady Shannon Crenshaw, or, I suppose it would be Lady Stamford." She shook her head. "Just call me Shannon."

"Oh? I never could," Miss Joyce said, hazel eyes going wide.

"We insist." Colin stepped in, extending his hand. "I am Colin, otherwise known as Lord Stamford, but only if you wish to annoy me."

"And this is my cousin, Lord Caelian O'Shea." Shannon smiled as she gestured to Caelian.

That smile grew even broader when Caelian simply gazed at the woman and said, "Hello."

"Hello," Miss Joyce said in return, smiling bashfully. The two of them stared at each other for a moment before Miss Joyce practically exploded with another,

"Oh! I am intruding. I am sorry, I do not wish to intrude. I should leave you now. But do feel free to attend services at St. Cuthbert's. I assist my father sometimes. And it would be lovely to get to know you better." She spoke ostensibly to Shannon, but her gaze slipped across to Caelian before she nodded, bowed, and curtsied all together, then rushed off as though she were still chasing her kite.

"Well, that was an unexpected diversion," Shannon said, grinning at Caelian.

Caelian continued to stare after Miss Joyce long after she disappeared back down to the beach. It was another few moments before he sucked in a breath, turned to Shannon and Colin, and asked, "I beg your pardon?"

Shannon grinned at Colin, who winked back at her. "Fergus might be crowing because he's married off all of his sisters, but it appears as though there are still more O'Sheas to matchmake for," she said.

"I do believe you are right, my beautiful wife," Colin said, stealing a kiss, even though Caelian was standing right there in front of him. Caelian wasn't paying attention to them, though. He'd gone back to staring at the horizon. Colin went on. "I think things are only just beginning to become interesting."

I HOPE YOU'VE ENJOYED SHANNON AND COLIN'S story! What Shannon said about women running the brewing industry in the Middle Ages is absolutely true, by the way. We tend to think that women owning businesses is a modern thing, but it absolutely wasn't. Brewing was only one female-owned industry that can be seen in history. There were plenty of others as well. In pre-industrial society, the entire family would be involved in whatever provided the income, from farming to weaving to soap-making. The Industrial Revolution went a long way toward separating men's and women's work, but in several cases, including one notable story about a female blacksmith in the late 1700s, if a husband died, his wife might very well take over the entire business.

As for That Wicked O'Shea Family, as you might have guessed, just because Fergus's sisters have all found their mates, that doesn't mean there aren't other family members to consider! What about Cousin Caelian and the mysterious Englishwoman, Erica Joyce? Will a humble preacher's daughter be a good match for an eccentric viscount and his dragon? ... By which I mean his *flying machine*, of course. Find out next in *All the Single Viscounts*.

If you enjoyed this book and would like to hear more from me, please sign up for my newsletter! When you sign up, you'll get a free, full-length novella, *A*

Passionate Deception. Victorian identity theft has never been so exciting in this story of hope, tricks, and starting over. Part of my West Meets East series, *A Passionate Deception* can be read as a stand-alone. Pick up your free copy today by signing up to receive my newsletter (which I only send out when I have a new release)!

Sign up here: http://eepurl.com/cbaVMH

ARE YOU ON SOCIAL MEDIA? I AM! COME AND JOIN the fun on Facebook: http://www.facebook.com/merryfarmerreaders

I'M ALSO A HUGE FAN OF INSTAGRAM AND POST LOTS of original content there: https://www.instagram.com/merryfarmer/

ABOUT THE AUTHOR

I hope you have enjoyed *Earls Just Wanna Have Fun*. If you'd like to be the first to learn about when new books in the series come out and more, please sign up for my newsletter here: http://eepurl.com/cbaVMH And remember, Read it, Review it, Share it! For a complete list of works by Merry Farmer with links, please visit http://wp.me/P5ttjb-14F.

Merry Farmer is an award-winning novelist who lives in suburban Philadelphia with her cats, Justine and Peter. She has been writing since she was ten years old and realized one day that she didn't have to wait for the teacher to assign a creative writing project to write something. It was the best day of her life. She then went on to earn not one but two degrees in History so that she would always have something to write about. Her books have reached the Top 100 at Amazon, iBooks, and Barnes & Noble, and have been named finalists in the prestigious RONE and Rom Com Reader's Crown awards.

ACKNOWLEDGMENTS

I owe a huge debt of gratitude to my awesome beta-readers, Caroline Lee and Jolene Stewart, for their suggestions and advice. And double thanks to Julie Tague, for being a truly excellent editor and to Cindy Jackson for being an awesome assistant!

Click here for a complete list of other works by Merry Farmer.

Printed in Great Britain
by Amazon